GHOST BUDDY

HOW TO SCARE THE PANTS OFF YOUR PETS

HENRY WINKLER
AND LIN OLIVER

SCHOLASTIC INC.

For all the children: Jed, Zoe, Max, Indya Belle,
and Ace, who keep my imagination young.
And for Stacey, always. — H.W.

For beautiful little Anarres, welcome to life!
— L.O.

ISBN 978-0-545-29884-1

12 11 10 9 8 7 6 5 4 3 2 1   13 14 15 16 17 18/0

Printed in the U.S.A.   40
First printing, January 2013

Designed by Steve Scott

CHAPTER 1

"AAAAAHHHHHHCHOOOOOOOOO!"

It was the sneeze heard around the world. Or if not the world, at least the neighborhood. And it didn't stop at one, either. It was followed by two more, each blast more powerful than the last. Billy Broccoli had never heard Hoover Porterhouse III sneeze before. In fact, he never even knew a ghost could sneeze, but apparently they can, and with the force of a hurricane.

"Holy moly," Billy said to the Hoove. "At least cover your mouth."

"I did," the Hoove answered. "But I blew my hand right off. That's the kind of power I possess. Besides, I can't help myself. My delicate system is allergic to paint fumes."

"Well, we're redoing my room this weekend, so you better get used to it."

Billy reached down and stirred the can of

paint his stepfather, Bennett Fielding, had just brought in. It was a medium shade of blue, dark enough to cover the pink-and-lavender night-mare walls Billy had been living with for the past eight weeks since his blended family had moved into the new house.

"And why wasn't I informed about this par-ticular painting situation?" the Hoove asked. "It happens to be more my room than yours. Don't make me remind you that I was the one who lived here ninety-nine years ago when this was nothing but an orange grove and a ranch house. I think I deserve to know when my room is being painted and when it isn't."

"How could I tell you? You haven't been around, as usual," Billy snapped. "I looked for you everywhere — behind every door, inside every drawer. I even checked the laundry hamper."

"And what gives you the impression that a young ghost with my dapper personal style would choose to hang out with soiled garments? Or worse yet, fold myself up in your under-wear drawer?"

"Because last time I looked for you, I found you all scrunched up in my jar of colored markers."

"If you don't want me in there, don't get the fruity-scented ones. I happen to enjoy the fresh aroma of the lemon-lime green and the strawberry red. The combination sends my nose on a field trip to Pleasureville."

Billy could see that this argument was going nowhere, so he turned his attention back to stirring the can of paint. The Hoove floated across the room, trying to keep his distance from the smell.

"I'm glad to see you getting right down to work, Bill," Bennett said as he came back in with a drop cloth, two rollers, and a brush for the trim. "Painting this room will be a very fulfilling experience for us. Like the kind of satisfaction I get from filling a cavity. There is nothing more exciting than bringing a tooth back to health."

Bennett Fielding was a dentist who lived for teeth, not to mention healthy gums. He could talk about them for hours — and often did at the dinner table, which made digestion a challenge for the other family members.

What Billy didn't notice as he stirred the paint was that the Hoove's nose was starting to twitch, gearing up for another massive sneeze. This one out-blasted the first three.

"AHHHHHHHHHHHCHOOOOOOOOOOOO OOOOOOOOOOOOOO!"

The gust of wind from the Hoove's sneeze was so strong it blew across the room like a tornado, taking off Bennett's hairpiece in the process. Bennett reached up to catch it, but it was already in midair, spinning like a Frisbee across Billy's room. It landed on the jar of Billy's markers.

"Well, I certainly won't be going back in there anytime soon," the Hoove said.

Billy was astonished. He hadn't known that his new stepfather was hair impaired . . . otherwise known as bald as a bowling ball.

"Wow, Bennett," he said, as he watched Bennett bolt for his wig. "I didn't know you were . . . uh . . . uh . . . you know . . . um . . ."

"Bald?" Bennett said.

"Yeah, that's the word I was looking for. Does my mom know?"

"Of course. She helped me pick out this new wig. Before we started dating, I wore a curly one, but she felt I looked too much like Clarence the Clown. Now she helps me apply the head tape. It's something we like to share in the mornings before coffee."

The Hoove made a gagging sound.

"Well, let me share this with you," he said. "I can no longer allow my essence to remain in this room. The very mention of hair tape on your stepdad's scalp makes me want to get as far away from his toupee as possible. Let's say, New Jersey."

"You can't leave now," Billy said. "You were going to help paint."

"And that's exactly why I'm here, son," Bennett said, thinking Billy was talking to him (which was a natural thing to think, since the Hoove was invisible to everyone but Billy). "Let's get started. Grab a roller, I'll do the same, and off we go."

"And off I go," the Hoove said, propelling himself out the window. It was a lovely day in Southern California. The Hoove floated over to the Brownstones' house next door, past the elaborate bed of Mrs. Brownstone's prize-winning hydrangeas and into the middle of the backyard, where he saw Rod Brownstone practicing making a citizen's arrest using his eight-year-old sister, Amber, as a pretend lawbreaker.

"Up against the wall," he barked at her. "Hands over your head."

"Okay, but you better not tickle me."

"I'm an officer of the law," Brownstone snapped. "We don't tickle people. It's a violation of the policeman's code. Now, you have the right to remain silent."

"Don't tell me to be silent, you big stupid gooney bird," Amber said. "This is America, and I'll talk when I want to. I can even scream. And I think I will."

She let out a piercing scream that almost sent the Hoove into a tailspin. It also alarmed a nearby lizard, who was sunning himself on a twig. The lizard was so frightened he bolted off the twig and scurried up Rod's pant leg.

"I'm being attacked," Rod screeched in a voice that was even louder than his sister's. "Somebody get this mini alligator off me."

"It's just a little lizard, you scaredy-pants." Amber laughed.

"Whatever it is, it has four legs running in circles around my kneecap, and I want each and every leg off me right now."

Amber was no help. She was laughing too hard. The Hoove found Brownstone's situation highly amusing as well. Rod was a real bully, and it was great to see that underneath his menacing exterior, he was a blubbering baby inside. The Hoove was lucky enough to spot a second lizard hanging on the stucco wall of the Brownstone house.

"Come with me, my fine four-legged friend," the Hoove said. He picked up the little reptile and flew over to where Rod was still whimpering. With an impish grin, he dropped the lizard on Rod's head, where it promptly burrowed into his thick black hair.

"Oh no, they're multiplying," Rod screamed, dropping to the ground and rolling around in the grass. "I hate creepy crawlers. Get these things off of me!"

"Sorry, buddy," the Hoove said as he drifted off down the block, feeling very satisfied with himself. "I'd love to help, but I got a movie to catch."

The Hoove was a big fan of the movies. Although he liked the stories, mostly he loved sitting in the dark where the Higher-Ups — the ghostly grade givers who decided whether he'd move on or remain grounded forever — had trouble finding him and didn't usually ask him to do anything. The movies were his escape from responsibility. Lucky for him, three screens of the Cineplex were within the boundary of where he was allowed to go.

Hoover floated up to the theatre to see what was playing, but he was disappointed with his choices. Screen One was showing some stupid romantic comedy. Screen Three had another kissy-face film that looked like it didn't even have a single car chase. Screen Seven was showing a black-and-white documentary on why zebras could not live in Iceland.

Reluctantly, he chose Screen Three and promised himself that he'd cover his eyes when the kissing started. Which didn't work out so well, because when he covered his eyes, he could still see through his own hands. That was one of the drawbacks of being a ghost. He did, however, get to sit next to a mother and her teenage daughter who were sharing a big tub of popcorn. Even though the Hoove couldn't eat it, he loved the aroma, and every now and then, he'd lean in to catch a whiff of it.

It wasn't long before the kissing started on-screen, and to amuse himself, the Hoove reached over and gently blew a wisp of the girl's hair.

"Stop it, Mom," she said in an annoyed voice.

Her mother didn't answer. She was busy watching the film's couple strolling hand in hand along a sandy beach saying gooey things to each other in gooey voices. When the woman turned to the guy and said, "The wet sand beneath my feet feels gooey . . . like my heart does for you," the Hoove reached out and blew on the girl's hair again.

"Mom, leave me alone," she snapped. "It's not funny. I'm not a little girl anymore."

"I don't like your tone of voice," her mother snapped back. "Keep that up and we're leaving."

The Hoove let out a belly laugh. He loved causing trouble.

But the Higher-Ups, who were constantly monitoring his behavior, were not laughing. They were not pleased with the Hoove. He had abandoned Billy as soon as he found out work was involved. He had taken advantage of Rod's fear of lizards. And now he'd gotten this girl in trouble with her mom. In their eyes, this was the behavior that had given him another failing grade in Responsibility to Others. As far as they were concerned, unless he could pass Responsibility, he would never earn his freedom and be able to travel outside of the boundaries he had lived in for the last ninety-nine years. And they decided it was time Hoover knew just how serious his situation was.

When the *I-love-you*s on the screen started to come fast and furious, and the violins in the background swelled to a deafening pitch, Hoover had had enough. He took one last sniff of the popcorn and floated out of the theatre.

As he circled the parking lot, the Hoove pondered what to do next. He didn't want to go back to the house yet because Billy and Bennett were probably still hard at work painting. He decided that maybe he'd float over to the hardware store and say hello to Sid, an older ghost who had worked there during his life and was spending eternity sorting different-size nuts and bolts into their proper bins.

The Hoove flew down Mammoth Street to Ventura Boulevard, where the hardware store was located. Suddenly, he ran smack into something. Yet when he looked up, he saw nothing. How could nothing feel like something? He backed up and tried again, but found that he thumped into an invisible wall. The third time he sailed higher into the air, thinking he would just float over whatever was blocking his path, but once again, he smacked his head into something solid.

"What's going on here?" he said to no one in particular.

"You're grounded," said a voice from below. He looked down and saw a brown sparrow on the pavement pecking at a piece of a discarded granola bar.

"Did you say something?" the Hoove asked the bird.

"Yeah," the bird answered. "I said you're grounded. They put up a wall here. That's why you can't go any farther."

"Who put up a wall?"

"Who do you think? The Higher-Ups."

"Wait. . . . are you one of them?"

"Use your eyes. I'm a sparrow. Let's just say I have friends in high places. And you might want to read this."

The bird lifted its wing and with its beak pulled out a note that was folded in the shape of a paper airplane. The minute the note was exposed to air, it puffed up and up and up, until it was the size of a jet-shaped watermelon. "Here it comes," the bird said, launching the note with its left wing. It sailed toward the Hoove, doing a series of backward triple loops in the air and leaving a glittering trail of silver smoke behind it that spelled out the words *Special Delivery!*

Fortunately, the Hoove had spent much of his life playing baseball and was a great catcher. He reached out and scooped the note out of the air before it collided with the street sign.

"You've got to work on your aim," he said to the bird.

"Oh yeah? Well, you've got a lot to work on yourself." Then the bird took off, flying through the invisible wall and soaring off out of sight into the sky.

Hoover opened the note. The paper was completely blank . . . at first. Then, with a sudden flash, sparkling silver letters appeared on the page.

"*Progress Report*," it said.

The Hoove looked up at the sky. "I just had one of these two weeks ago," he hollered. "Don't you guys have anything better to do?"

There was another flash of light, and more words appeared on the page. They said:

"*You are hereby notified that as of this second, your boundaries have shrunk. You will return to the Broccoli-Fielding house immediately, and you will not be allowed to leave until we see marked improvement in your ability to accept responsibility.*"

"You can't do this to me!" the Hoove shouted defiantly into the sky.

He put his head down and charged into the invisible wall, thinking he could power his way through it, but as hard as he tried, it was impossible. He was going nowhere.

"Fine, I'll go the other way," he shouted. And he took off in the other direction, sailing down toward Moorepark Middle School, until he bumped up against another invisible wall. No matter which direction he tried to go, walls popped up to stop him. He felt like a caged animal. The only direction he could go was back toward Billy's house.

"I can't believe this," the Hoove shouted into the air. "I am the picture of responsibility. My middle name is Responsibility. I couldn't be any more responsible."

The small sparrow flew in from nowhere and perched on the Hoove's shoulder.

"Trust me, you're not going to win this one. I used to be a bald eagle, and look what they did to me."

"Yeah, well, they can't turn me into a scrawny feathered thing. I'm Hoover Porterhouse the Third, the ghost with the most, in case you hadn't noticed."

"Oh yeah. Well, notice this, tough guy."

And with that, the bird hunkered down, deposited a drippy dropping on the Hoove's shoulder, then spread its wings and disappeared into the distance.

"Okay," the Hoove called out to the sky. "So I'm grounded. You win round one. But you haven't heard the last of me! Oh, and by the way, where do I send the cleaning bill?"

CHAPTER 2

"Billy, we've got to talk," the Hoove said as he zoomed in through the window of Billy's room. "I have an urgent situation here that is completely unacceptable for ghost or human."

Billy and Dr. Fielding had finished painting two of the four walls. With half the walls a medium blue and the other half a screaming lavender, the room looked like a sunset over the Pacific Ocean. Dr. Fielding, of course, was unaware of the Hoove's abrupt entrance, but did notice that Billy had stopped painting and seemed to be staring at the window.

"Bill, attention to the task at hand," he gently reprimanded. "Daydreaming never gets anything accomplished. Do you think Henry Ford would have perfected the automobile if he allowed himself to daydream? No, he would have stopped at three wheels and ended up with a tricycle."

"Billy," the Hoove interrupted. "Can you tell this guy to take a lunch break? We have got to talk . . . now."

Billy put down his roller and wiped his hands on the rag in his back pocket.

"Hey, Bennett, if it's okay with you, I'm going to take a fruit juice break. I'll be back in ten minutes."

"Make that seven minutes, Bill. Remember the tricycle."

"Absolutely, Bennett. I'll be right back with that fourth wheel. And I'm going to look into power steering while I'm gone."

Bennett threw his head back and let out a big belly laugh.

"I like your sense of humor, Bill."

"Thanks, Ben. I like that you like it."

"Will you wrap up this lovefest and come with me right now," Hoover snapped. "I have a major problem that happens to be life altering. At least, it would be if I were alive."

The Hoove flew through the door and passed by Billy's stepsister Breeze's room, where she was hunched over her guitar with a pencil in her teeth and a notepad by her side, writing a new song for her band, the Dark Clouds.

"Did somebody just open the window?" she said as he flew by. "It suddenly got freezing in here."

"Sorry, Breeze," Billy called to his stepsister. "It'll warm up in a minute."

The Hoove was so agitated that the cold wind that followed him everywhere he went was even more intense than usual. As he passed Billy's mother, who was making tuna salad in the kitchen, she pulled her cardigan sweater a little tighter around her.

"The weather report didn't mention it was going to be this chilly," she commented to Billy as he ran into the kitchen. "Oh and, honey, while you're here, will you taste this tuna? I'm not sure the tuna to mayonnaise ratio is right."

"This is no time to be calling your taste buds into action," the Hoove yelled from the back door. "Outside, pronto."

Billy gulped down the tuna, told his mom it was perfect (which it was), then followed the Hoove through the laundry room, out the door, and down the steps that led to the backyard.

"Let's go back by the tree," Billy suggested, "so my mom won't see me talking to the air. That never works out for me very well."

Billy jogged across the backyard and turned around to see if the Hoove was following him. He wasn't. He was still only halfway across the yard. It looked like he was trying to glide forward but something was preventing him.

"What are you waiting for?" Billy asked.

"This is the problem I was referring to," the Hoove answered. "You're seeing it right here."

"Hoove, I'm going to need a little more explanation than that."

"I'm grounded," he said. "Stuck in, and I guess just outside, the house until further notice."

"What'd you do?"

"Nothing. I was just doing what I always do. And suddenly the Higher-Ups send this bird down with a note that says I'm failing Responsibility to Others. And I might add, that bird had a major digestive problem."

"So how long are you going to be punished for?"

"Who knows? Until they see improvement, they said. And let's get one thing straight: There is no room for improvement here. I am already the picture of perfection."

"According to you."

"That's right. The Hoove's Rule Number Seven is, 'When you're in the presence of perfection, bow to it.' Which I would do, but I can't lean forward without slamming into this annoying invisible wall."

Billy walked over to where the Hoove was suspended in midair. He reached out but didn't feel any obstruction. "Are you sure you're not making this up?"

"Allow me to demonstrate."

The Hoove backed up all the way to the screen door. Then, flying forward with all his might, he came to an abrupt stop halfway across the yard. He tried it again, leading with his shoulder the way a football player charges his opponent. At exactly the same spot, he slammed up against some invisible barrier.

"Are you seeing what I mean," he asked Billy, "or do I need to keep doing this until I'm black and blue?"

"I didn't know ghosts could get black and blue."

"I was trying to relate to you on a flesh level you could understand. Apparently, I misjudged."

"Okay, okay, I get the point."

"Yeah, well here's the real point, Billy Boy. What do I do about it?"

"Well, I remember when I was in fifth grade and I got caught littering on the lunch yard. The lunchroom monitors said I had to clean off all the lunch tables for two weeks. I can't tell you how many half-eaten peanut butter sandwiches I had to toss out. The thing about peanut butter is it gets stuck under your fingernails and you can smell it all day."

"I hope you're not suggesting that my road to responsibility will require handling used food. That's not the way I roll. I have sixty-seven rules about that, and that's not even including the ones about touching used napkins."

"All I'm saying is maybe you need to rewrite your rules. The Higher-Ups don't seem to be joking around."

The Hoove flopped down on one of the red-and-white-striped chaise lounges on the patio. It wasn't often that he felt defeated, but he was up against something too difficult for him to over-come. Billy sat down on the striped chair opposite the chaise. He actually felt bad for the Hoove.

"Hey, this is not rocket science," he said. "You're just going to have to make some better choices in how you behave. You know, show the Higher-Ups that you understand what it takes to be responsible to others."

"What am I supposed to do? Go around help-ing old ladies across the street? If I did that, Billy Boy, there would be an epidemic of faint-ing in Senior Citizen Land. That would get me an F for sure."

"Why don't you just ask the Higher-Ups what they expect of you? That's what I did with Mr. Wallwetter when I flunked my vocabulary test. He said he expected me to know the defini-tion of the word *indigenous*."

"And?"

"I couldn't spell it, so I couldn't look it up. I flunked the test again, but at least I knew what he wanted."

"Would you be very offended if I told you your adventures in vocabulary not only do not appeal to me, they do not pertain to me and, simply put, are of no help at all. But thank you for that boring story."

The screen door creaked open and Bennett stuck his head out. He checked his wristwatch.

"Six and a half minutes have elapsed . . . right . . . now!" he said. "By my calculations, that gives us thirty seconds to hustle down the hall and resume painting. And to continue those precise calculations, we have two and a half walls down and one and a half to go."

"It appears Mr. I'm - Really - Good - With - Fractions doesn't care that we're talking here," the Hoove grumbled.

Billy followed Bennett back into the house. The two of them worked the rest of the afternoon to finish the painting job. Since the Hoove couldn't tolerate the paint smell, he hovered in the hall, calling out comments and critiques.

"Hey, you missed a spot up there by the ceiling," he'd shout. Then two minutes later, he'd add, "And tell the dentist there that I can see his butt crack peeking out when he bends over. And it's making my eyes nauseous."

Billy shot the Hoove a look that said, "I wish you'd get lost." Several times, the Hoove left and wandered around the house, trying to amuse himself. When Mrs. Broccoli-Fielding was downstairs in the laundry room, he took the stack of student absence records she had just alphabetized and shuffled them like a deck of cards. Then he went into Breeze's room and floated over to the dresser where she kept her vast collection of nail polish bottles. When she wasn't looking, he took a bottle of yellow and poured in some blue, leaving her with a bottle of pond-scum-green nail polish. Of all of his pranks, he found that one the most entertaining.

When he could think of no other mischief to get into, the Hoove floated back to Billy's room, where Billy and Bennett had just finished painting the last wall. They stood back and admired their work.

"I'm so glad to get rid of all that girly lavender and pink," Billy said. "Thanks for making this a priority, Bennett. I know you must have had better things to do with your weekend."

"Yes, I was going to carve every tooth in the adult mouth out of soap and string them into a necklace for your mom," Bennett said. "But then I thought, Bill needs me, and his room needs me even more."

"The man is tooth obsessed," the Hoove said, floating into the room to check out the paint job. "Does the subject of molars ever leave his brain? Wait a minute, wind warning!"

His invisible nose started to twitch, and he took several of his invisible fingers and tried to pinch it hard to stop what was coming. But the sneeze had a mind of its own.

"Ahchoooooooooooooo!"

The sneeze came out with such a powerful gust that it actually blew the paintbrush that was balanced on the top of the can halfway across the room. Bennett looked around, puzzled.

"Did you open a window, Bill? That was quite a gust of air."

"Uh . . . no . . . Bennett. It was me sighing. I know it was a big sigh, but I always let out a big sigh when I've finished a major project. You should have heard the one when I finished my term paper on the Bermuda Triangle. I practically launched that green T-shirt over there like a kite."

"That was a whopper, Billy Boy," the Hoove called out. "I've heard a lot of excuses in my ninety-nine years as a ghost, and that is definitely in the top ten."

"Thanks," Billy said.

"You're welcome," Bennett answered. "That's what families do, help each other. Which is why I'm sure Breeze won't mind that you spend a couple nights in her room."

"What?" Billy said. "She's going to hate that."

"Well you certainly can't sleep in here with all the paint fumes. We'll move the guest futon into Breeze's room. It'll give you two a chance to get to know each other a little better."

Needless to say, the news did not go over well with Breeze.

"You're kidding me, right, Dad? You expect me to share my personal space with a sixth grader who drools small puddles all over his pillow when he sleeps?"

"It's not my fault," Billy answered. "My nose gets congested when I'm lying down, and I have to breathe through my mouth."

"Breeze, Billy is your new brother, and I really need you to cooperate," Bennett said sternly. "It's just for a few days."

After laying down the law, Bennett turned and left. He'd argued with Breeze often enough to know that a speedy escape was the only way to end the conversation.

"A few days to you is a lifetime to me," Breeze hollered after him. Then she suddenly stopped talking and grabbed a pencil. "Wait a minute," she said. "That's a great title for a song. I can already hear my guitar solo. . . . It'll be tragic, but with a great beat."

"Has anyone consulted me in this matter?" Hoover said. Billy looked up to see him pacing back and forth upside down on the ceiling of Breeze's room. "The answer is absolutely not. The Hoove's Rule Number Two Hundred and Forty-Three: I do not share rooms with girls who sound like injured cats when they sing. End of discussion."

"Where else are you going to go?" Billy whispered to him. "In our room, you'd sneeze your nose off, if you had a nose."

"What are you talking about?" Breeze said,

giving Billy a puzzled look. "Of course I have a nose. I have a great nose, unlike yours, which reminds me of Mount Kilimanjaro."

"Listen, Breeze, there's no need to get personal. I'm not crazy about this arrangement, either, but we're going to have to make the best of it."

Without answering, Breeze picked up her guitar and started to compose her new song. It was rough on the ears.

"Can you tell her to pipe down?" the Hoove called from inside the closet. "I'm trying to take a snooze before dinner."

But there was no telling Breeze what she could or couldn't do in her own room. Billy helped Bennett move the futon in while she continued to compose, playing the same rotten notes over and over again. Inside the closet, the Hoove was going bananas. He tried stuffing his ears with her velvet scarves, but nothing could drown out the sound.

Breeze continued writing until she finished her song. When it was done, she cleared her throat and sang the lyrics at the top of her terrible voice.

A few days to you is a lifetime to me,
A feeling of heartbreak for eternity.
I roam and I search and I wail for you,
But nothing will fill this hole in my shoe.

From inside the closet, the Hoove held his head and moaned. Getting grounded was going to be much worse than he had ever imagined.

CHAPTER 3

Billy walked into Breeze's room after dinner to find her standing on a chair, trying to attach one end of a bungee cord to the curtain rod. The other end was already attached to the top of her doorjamb. She was having a hard time, because the cord was already stretched to its limit.

"What's going on here?" Billy asked.

The sound of his voice so startled Breeze that she let go of the cord. It boomeranged across the room, making a snapping sound as it sailed through the air, and just missed Billy's nose by the length of a pencil eraser.

"Whoa," he said, as he dropped to the rug. "Watch what you're doing, Breeze. That's a dangerous weapon you've got there. What are you doing with it, anyway?"

"I'm creating a boundary line."

"With a bungee cord?"

"It's not finished, doofus. I'm going to string the bungee across my room, then hang a sheet over it. You will stay on your side of the sheet at all times and can only cross over to my side of the room if you say the secret password."

"Okay, this is ridiculous, but I'll play along. What is it?"

"That's for me to know and you to find out."

Breeze got off the chair and retrieved the other end of the bungee. This time, she successfully hooked it onto the curtain rod. Then she went to the linen closet and brought back two sheets with pink ballerina mice dancing all over them.

"You're putting those up?" Billy commented. "I can't look at pink mice all night."

"These were my favorite sheets when I was your age. Seven."

"You really know how to hurt a guy, hitting him with a marshmallow like that."

Breeze didn't answer. She was already busy throwing the sheets over the bungee cord and making sure they touched the floor so Billy couldn't see a thing on her side. The Hoove, who had just woken up from his long nap, stuck his head through the closet keyhole and surveyed the scene.

"Is she serious?" he said to Billy. "Because if she is, she is seriously misguided. Hoover Porterhouse the Third does not stick to anyone's boundaries but his own. And certainly not those established by girls with blue streaks in their hair."

"Seems to me the Higher-Ups have another opinion about you and boundaries," Billy whispered.

"Those don't count," the Hoove said. "They're just temporary until I show them who's boss."

Suddenly, a clap of thunder boomed so loud it made the windows rattle.

"Where did that come from?" Breeze shrieked. "There's not a cloud in the sky."

Billy looked over at the Hoove.

"I think the Higher-Ups are talking to you, buddy. You might want to show a little respect."

When the sheets were hung to Breeze's satisfaction, she pushed them aside to enter Billy's side of the room.

"These are my conditions," she began, clearing her throat as if she were an actress on a stage. "First, this is my room and you touch nothing in it, especially my guitar. It's the instrument by which I express my soul and no one handles it but me."

"Maybe someone should tell her that her soul is out of tune," the Hoove commented.

"Second, you are to breathe as little air in here as possible. I would appreciate you exhaling in the direction of the door. I don't want my room polluted by your pizza breath."

"Breeze, I haven't had pizza in a week," Billy protested.

"You wouldn't know it from the pepperoni and garlic aroma that follows you like a cloud."

"Billy Boy," the Hoove said, floating completely out of the closet and coming right up to him. "You're not going to take this abuse, are you? Because this girl is really razzing my berries."

"Furthermore," Breeze continued, "there's no eating or drinking in my room. So tell me now where you're hiding the orange juice."

"I don't have any, Breeze. Honest."

"It smells like you brought the orange tree from the front yard in here."

Billy had no good answer for Breeze's complaint. He couldn't tell the truth. The Hoove always smelled like oranges, because when the property had been the Porterhouse ranchero, he'd spent lots of time wandering around their orange groves. And when he got riled up, his odor got even more intense and tangy.

"I don't know what you're talking about," Billy said. "You can conduct a search of my person if you like, and I promise you won't find an orange or a grapefruit or any other fruit known to mankind. So is that your third condition . . . no eating or drinking?"

"No, that's a subsection B footnote," Breeze answered. "My actual third condition is that you can only be in here when you're asleep. No hanging out in an awake state."

This did it for the Hoove. He had reached his limit of taking orders from Breeze. He felt like he was on the verge of exploding.

"I can't take this anymore," he said to Billy. "She is not the boss of us. So stand back and observe as a master rule breaker moves her precious guitar and hangs it from the light fixtures. Let's see how she likes them apples."

"No! You can't do that!" Billy said in a loud voice.

"Can't do what?" Breeze answered. "Let me remind you, youngster, that this is my room and I can do whatever I please, which includes demanding that you turn your ears off when I'm on the phone."

As Breeze went on to explain the dos and don'ts of living in her room, the Hoove drifted over to her guitar, lifted it off its stand, and, flying up to the light fixture on the ceiling, hung the guitar from its tie-dyed strap. It seemed to be floating in midair.

"Hey, music babe," the Hoove called out. "Take a gander at this. It's a doozy."

Of course, Breeze couldn't hear the Hoove or see what he had done, but Billy could. As he looked in shock at the guitar hanging from the ceiling, his mouth flew open in horror. Seeing his reaction, Breeze turned around and gasped when she saw that her beloved instrument had been moved.

"What part of 'don't touch it' do you not understand?" she screamed directly into Billy's face. And without waiting for an answer, she jumped on her bed and reached up to take her guitar down, cradling it in her arms like a baby.

"That's it," she said to Billy. "You haven't even been in my room for six minutes and already you have broken my most important rule. I am declaring an end to room sharing right here, right now."

She put her guitar back on its stand, then stomped over to the futon. She bent down and grabbed hold of the mattress. Yanking it with all her might, she dragged it through her door and into the hallway, letting it plop down against the wall. Billy followed her out into the hall.

"Say hello to your new guest quarters," she said.

"I can't sleep out here, and you know it."

Without a word, Breeze marched back into her room and answered him by slamming the door so hard that it created enough wind to mess up Billy's hair. The Hoove floated through the door, holding his sides and laughing up a storm.

"Did you see the look on her face?" he howled. "We showed her a thing or two."

"And what exactly did we show her, Hoove? That I get to sleep in the hall?"

"Oh, come on, it was worth it. We didn't let her push us around. I feel very good about that and you should, too."

"What should I feel good about? That I'm sleeping in the hall? That I get to go to school tomorrow wiped out, with dark circles under my eyes?"

"You are missing the point, William. We took care of business. Who cares if you miss one night of sleep?"

"I care. I happen to have a math quiz tomorrow that I was hoping to do well on."

"The problem with you, Billy Boy, is that you're so responsible. Who cares about a math quiz? You've got to lighten up a little."

"The problem with you, Hoove, is that you're not responsible enough! If you looked up Hoover Porterhouse the Third in the dictionary, it would say *irresponsible*."

"I disagree with your definition. I think it would say *handsome*. Or *dashing*. Or both."

"No wonder the Higher-Ups are flunking you in Responsibility."

"This conversation has taken a boring turn." The Hoove yawned. "So if you'll excuse me, I will retire and snooze it up on the ceiling-fan blade."

"Oh, sure, you can sleep anywhere," Billy said to the Hoove. "But not me. I'm going to fail my math quiz. I have to listen to the toilet flush all night. And all because of you. You and your lack of responsibility are driving me crazy."

"Let me remind you, William, that you're not a perfect peach, either."

The Hoove floated up to the ceiling and stretched himself out on a blade of the hall ceiling fan. He put his hands behind his head, let out a loud yawn, and said, "Hey, this is a first for me. In all my ninety-nine years, I've never slept on a fan. And you know what . . . it's kind of cozy up here."

Down below, Billy paced back and forth in the little aisle that was left between the futon and the wall. He was furious at the Hoove. He dropped to his knees on the futon and pounded the mattress with all his might.

"Hey, do you mind keeping it down?" the Hoove called out. "Some of us have to get our beauty rest."

"I swear, Hoove, if it's the last thing I do, I'm going to figure out some way to stuff responsibility down your nonexistent throat."

"You do that, buddy. In the meantime, I'm going to get some shut-eye. Though it'd be a lot easier if I had eyelids."

The Hoove guffawed at his own joke, then fell immediately asleep.

Not Billy. He paced back and forth, trying to figure out how to teach a ghost to be responsible. By the time the sun came up, he still hadn't found an answer.

CHAPTER 4

Billy had a miserable night. The lack of sleep and his impending math quiz thrust him into the grumpiest mood of the century. When he brushed his teeth the next morning, he gargled with a vengeance. He didn't even bother to change his clothes. All he did was scrub under his arms with soap without ever taking off his shirt. Slipping into his sneakers, he stomped into the kitchen, where Bennett was preparing some sunny-side-up eggs.

"Hey, Bill," Bennett grinned. "Sit yourself down and fortify yourself for the day with a hearty meal. Nothing like Dr. Fielding's Fabulous Fried Eggs to give your system the proper jump start."

"Thanks but no thanks, Bennett. I'm too tired to be hungry."

"Hey, you were warned," Breeze said, shuffling into the kitchen in her Australian sheepskin slippers. "I told him, Dad. I said, 'Touch my guitar, and the hand of doom will slap you silly.'"

"Well, the hand of doom didn't have to toss me in the hall," Billy said. "You see these eyes? See how bloodshot they are? That's because they didn't close for a second all night."

"Oh really?" Breeze said, full of fake concern as she slipped into her chair at the breakfast table. "I'm so sorry to hear that. I got a great night's sleep."

Bennett put the plate of eggs in front of Breeze.

"You kids have to try to get along when you have conflict," he said. "Take the human mouth, for example. It contains all kinds of teeth and yet they all work together to get the chewing done. Bicuspids, incisors, molars . . ."

"Enough, Dad," Breeze interrupted. "My wisdom teeth got the point. He touched my property, he had to pay."

"Well, there will be no more sleeping in the hall," Bennett said. "It's *un*fair, *un*heatlthy, and *un*called for."

"You forgot the major *un*," Billy chimed in. "*Un*comfortable."

"I think it's safe for you to go back into your own room tonight," Bennett said. "We'll leave the windows open and the paint fumes should be gone by bedtime."

"Too bad," Breeze said to Billy. "It was nice rooming with you."

"Wish I could say the same," Billy answered, picking up his lunch and putting it in his backpack. He grabbed a piece of toast and headed for the door.

"If you want a lift, your mother should be leaving for school in five minutes," Bennett offered.

"I need to walk," Billy answered. "Maybe some fresh air will wake up my math brain cells."

Before Bennett could get his usual "Have a great day" out of his mouth, Billy was out the door and down the stairs, crossing the backyard toward the sidewalk. On the way, he ran into Amber Brownstone, Rod Brownstone's eight-year-old sister. She was carrying a small plastic cage with a mesh front.

"Hi, Billy," she called out. "Want to say hello to Mr. Claws? He's excited to meet you."

She came running over to Billy and shoved the cage in front of his face. Billy looked inside and saw a pink, hairless creature with gray whiskers and two long front teeth that made whatever it was look like a mini beaver.

"What exactly do you call that animal, besides ugly?" he asked Amber, trying hard not to throw up at the sight of the weirdly wrinkled pink skin.

"He's a hairless rat," she said. "Isn't he cute? We love each other."

"Wow. My mom always says there's somebody for everybody. Lucky that you and Mr. Claws found each other."

"Do you want to hold him?"

"That would be a firm no," Billy said as he hurried out of the backyard to the sidewalk. Amber followed close behind him.

"Do you mind if we walk to school with you?" she said. "I'm not allowed to walk by myself, and my brother doesn't get along with Mr. Claws so he won't walk me to school today."

"Whatever," Billy said. "Just make sure Mr. Claws keeps his distance."

"Mom!" Amber yelled in a surprisingly loud voice for a little girl. "I'm going to school with Billy Broccoli. See you later."

"Thank you, Billy," Mrs. Brownstone called out from inside the house. "You're such a nice boy. Just remember to look both ways before you cross the street."

Billy stepped onto the pavement, trying not to look too closely at Mr. Claws. He wasn't a big fan of bald animals. Once, he had a parakeet named Leo that lost all its feathers. Leo was so embarrassed about it that he constantly dive-bombed at Billy's ear lobes. Ever since then, Billy had demanded that any animals he was around be covered in whatever nature intended them to be covered in.

"Mr. Claws is going to school with me because it's Pet Day," Amber rambled on. "Everyone has to share their pets and tell the class how we take care of them."

"Did you warn them about Mr. Claws's fur-less condition? Some people might be shocked," Billy commented.

"Oh no. Everybody loves Mr. Claws. He's very social."

"Like how?" Billy asked. "Does he dress up for dances, or take girl rats to the movies?"

Amber laughed so hard her eyes watered.

"You're such a silly Billy," she said. "I wish my brother, Rod, was funny like you. All he does is report me to my parents for behavior infractions, whatever they are. He says they're in the police codebook, which I won't even be able to read until the fourth grade. Mr. Claws and I get really frustrated with him, don't we, Mr. Claws?"

Billy and Amber stopped at the corner and waited for the crossing guard to hold up her WALK sign. Meanwhile, Amber chattered on . . . and on . . . and on. Billy could hardly wait for the light to turn green.

"It's a lot of responsibility to have a pet," she pointed out. "I mean, Mr. Claws depends on me to feed him and clean up his cage and give him water and fresh wood chips, which he uses for a comfy bed. But I like taking care of him."

"Why?" Billy asked. Something in what she was saying was stirring his curiosity.

"Because it makes me feel good. And it makes me feel grown up. My teacher, Ms.

Glockworth, says that learning to be responsible is the most important part of growing up."

The light changed, and the crossing guard came to take them across the street. Amber rambled on, but Billy had stopped listening. Instead, he was thinking about what Amber had said. Taking care of a pet was a great way to learn responsibility. And who needed responsibility badly?

The Hoove, that's who.

Billy smiled to himself all the rest of the way to Moorepark Middle School. He was already planning his after-school schedule. A peanut butter and strawberry jelly sandwich on toasted wheat. A glass of Bennett's homemade pink lemonade. And a trip to Fur 'N Feathers Pet Store.

Billy could barely keep his eyes open all day at school. He yawned so loudly in English class that Mr. Wallwetter thought he was answering a question about semicolons. During his math quiz, he nodded off in the middle of a word problem. And in PE, when he lay down on the soccer field during halftime, he got a lecture from the coach about the importance of staying upright during the game. But by the time the final bell rang at three o'clock, he got a sudden surge of energy at the thought of implementing his new plan. He felt that he had discovered the key to helping the Hoove learn to be responsible and he couldn't wait to put it into action — not just for the Hoove, but for himself. It was no fun living with a grounded ghost.

Billy hurried home and flew through the back door, heading straight for the peanut butter and jelly. Before he could even drop the two pieces of bread into the toaster, he felt a cold draft behind him and smelled the distinct aroma of tart orange juice. Then he heard the whistling of "I've Been Working on the Railroad," which could only mean one thing. The Hoove was in the kitchen and making his presence known.

"It's about time you got home," Hoover snarled. "Do you know what it's like being locked up in this house all day with just your single self?"

"I thought you'd find yourself so interesting and entertaining that the day would just fly by."

"Even for a fascinating person such as myself, eight hours is a long time to be alone in this house, unless you're the type of person who wants to spend your time browsing Bennett's collection of antique tooth extracting equipment, which I am definitely not."

Billy opened the peanut butter jar, got out a knife, and started to make his sandwich. He didn't even cast a glance in the Hoove's direction, which infuriated the Hoove even more.

"I'm not feeling any sympathy for my situation coming from your direction," he snapped.

"Oh really? I didn't hear any sympathy coming from your direction when I was trying to fall asleep in the hallway all night."

"Apples and oranges, Billy Boy. You and I are not alike."

"The thing about you, Hoove, is that you can't see anyone else's problems, you only see your own. That's why it's so hard for you to be responsible to other people. But I have a fix for that."

"Don't you think you should discuss it with me, your life coach?"

"No. You don't have a choice about this. I have to get you ungrounded. Not just for you, but for me, too. And I think I know the perfect way to do it."

"So what do you have in mind?"

"You'll find out soon enough," Billy said, slapping the jelly-covered bread slice on top of the peanut butter slice. As he grabbed his sandwich and shot out the back door, the Hoove tried to follow him, but bumped smack into another invisible barrier.

"Whatever you got up your sleeve, you better pull it out fast," he yelled to Billy. "Because I cannot take one more minute of this."

In his frustration, the Hoove picked up a patio chair and tossed it onto the lawn.

"You can't break my spirit," he shouted up to the sky. "There's not a wall in the world that can contain Hoover Porterhouse the Third."

Suddenly, a black cloud appeared overhead and shot a bolt of lightning so close to his feet that he could feel its heat.

"I was just joking," he hollered to the Higher-Ups. "You guys have no sense of humor."

Another bolt of lightning shot out of the sky and burned the word *enough* into the grass. If Hoover Porterhouse needed proof that those Higher-Ups weren't kidding, this was certainly it.

CHAPTER 5

Billy walked up and down the aisles of Fur 'N Feathers Pet Store, his ears filled with the sounds of the animals in every section. Parakeets chirped, lovebirds cooed, and parrots squawked. Puppies yelped, cats meowed, and if you had very good ears, you could even hear the sound of snakes slithering across the sand at the bottom of their glass terrariums. He was so involved in looking into every cage, that the sound of the store owner's voice almost sent him flying out of his shoes.

"I can sense it," she said to Billy. "Can you?"

Billy turned to her and was about to ask what she meant, but she put a finger up to her lips.

"Shhh, listen. I can hear the buzz of excitement. Everyone here is so happy you're in the shop, and they all want to get to know you. Who would you like to meet first? Oh, why don't we start with me? I'm Daisy Cole."

"Nice to meet you, Ms. Cole."

"Call me Daisy — everyone does."

From a perch over the cash register, a gray parrot squawked, "Daisy. Daisy."

"See, I wasn't kidding," Daisy laughed. "That's Robert over there on the perch. He and I have been together since he was an egg. Isn't that right, Bobby, honey?"

Robert didn't answer in words. Instead, he burst into a rollicking chorus of "You Ain't Nothing But a Hound Dog." Daisy laughed.

"That Robert, he's a big Elvis Presley fan," she giggled. "He's got great rhythm for a parrot, don't you think?"

Billy didn't really have much of an opinion about that, since he didn't know any other singing parrots to compare him with.

"Is this your shop, Daisy?" he asked, swiftly changing the subject.

"Oh, this isn't a shop, this is a play space for all my creature friends. Now, how can I help you?"

"Well, my name is Billy Broccoli, and I've recently moved into the neighborhood."

"Don't tell me, you're looking for a puppy for your new house."

"Soon, maybe, but not today. I need something in a smaller size that would help teach this person I know to be responsible to others."

"Can I assume we're talking about a brother or sister?"

"Definitely, absolutely, without a doubt, no. This guy is no relation to me. I think of him more as a project."

"Well, that's a very thoughtful thing for a friend to do."

"I didn't say he was a friend, either. He kind of just floats around my house being a pain in the neck."

"So he'll need a soothing pet, one that will keep him calm. I have just the thing."

Daisy clopped down the aisle in her red patent leather clogs. At the sound of her footsteps, all the animals started to yelp, bark, meow, squawk, chirp, or whatever else they did . . . and scampered up to the front of their enclosures.

They were happy to see Daisy, and she was thrilled to see them, too.

"Hi, Freddy! Hello, Andrea! I love you, too, Buttercup!" she sang as she walked down the aisle. Her enthusiasm was boundless, and as Billy followed her, he found himself feeling warmth for every animal he saw, including the snakes . . . which would normally have given him a large dose of the creeps. At the end of the aisle, Daisy stopped at a glass tank, where a dark brown creature with a white stripe down its back was standing perfectly still on a green branch. She turned to Billy and smiled.

"Meet Berko," she beamed. "He's a fat-tailed gecko."

"Doesn't it hurt Berko's feelings when you call his tail fat?"

Daisy laughed again, and when she did, Robert the parrot imitated the sound of her giggle exactly, which set off all the other animals. It was like a laugh factory in there.

"Fat-tailed gecko is the name of this species," Daisy explained. "They store their fat in their tails. If they lose their tail in a fight, they grow another one, but often it looks more like a head than a tail."

"Sounds borderline disgusting," Billy said. "And the reason I'd want this guy as a pet is why, exactly?"

"Berko is very calm. He sleeps through the night, and as you can see, he has such soulful eyes. Sometimes I wonder what deep thoughts are running through his sweet little lizard brain."

"Maybe that a fly would taste delicious right about now," Billy suggested.

"Actually, it's probably a cricket he's craving. Berko loves crickets, don't you, Berkie, honey. Yes, you are mommy's little hungry lizard."

Billy bent down and stared into Berko's soulful eyes, trying to see even one deep thought rolling around in there. But all he saw was his own reflection staring back at him from Berko's shiny black eyeballs.

"Hey, Berko," he began. "How would you like to come home with me?"

Berko shot out his tongue. Apparently, he didn't quite understand how long it was, because it smashed into the glass and bent at a ninety-degree angle.

"Easy there, buddy. I'm not a cricket."

"Berko was just giving you a high-tongue-five," Daisy said. "It's his way of saying yes. He's such a positive little gecko."

Billy looked closely at Berko, wondering if this was an animal the Hoove could get along with. He didn't seem to require much care, which was a good thing, because the Hoove was going to have to ease into responsibility. Billy knew the Hoove certainly couldn't start off with a pet like a rabbit, which required a lot of care, especially cleaning up those pellets that seemed to fall fairly frequently from the area under their cute little cotton tails. And Daisy had said that Berko was very calm and slept through the night. That worked well with Hoover Porterhouse's Rule Number 26, "Never disturb my beauty sleep."

"How much is he?" Billy asked Daisy. "I only have twelve dollars and forty-three cents."

"That is amazing," Daisy exclaimed, clapping her chubby hands together in delight, "because this particular gecko is on sale this week for *exactly* that amount!"

"What about his tank?" Billy asked.

"If you promise to take good care of my little Berko, I'll throw that in for free. Plus, two delicious crickets that will last him for one week."

"I can't thank you enough for this deal," Billy said to Daisy.

"I'm always happy to find a good home for one of my little darlings," Daisy said. "You have to promise to come back soon and tell me how Berko and your friend are getting along."

Daisy transferred Berko, his water dish, his green branch, and a plastic rock cave into a smaller glass tank, and then walked up and down the aisles so that Berko could say goodbye to all of his creature friends.

"Everyone wish him well," she called out, and hearing that, Robert burst into a chorus of "I Left My Heart in San Francisco." Berko wasn't going to San Francisco, but try explaining that to a parrot.

As Billy walked home carrying the tank, he wanted to explain to Berko what he was about to encounter. Of course, he knew a fat-tailed gecko wouldn't understand what he was saying, but he thought maybe Berko could pick up something from his tone of voice.

"The Hoove is a ghost," he said slowly and patiently as he walked down Moorepark Avenue, past the dry cleaners and Hugo's taco stand. "He can have a bit of an attitude, so just be really friendly and give him time to adjust to you."

Some of the customers at Hugo's were giving Billy strange looks, so he stopped talking. When he reached his house, he took Berko in through the back door so he could go directly to his room undetected.

"Hoove," he whispered as he kicked the door open with his foot. "Are you here? I've got an amazing surprise for you!"

Billy looked around and didn't see anything but the new blue walls and an open window. As he put the tank down on top of his desk, he heard the whistling of "I've Been Working on the Railroad" and one second later, half of the Hoove appeared perched on the windowsill. It was as if he was split right down the center. He looked at Billy with one eye, which was the only one that was visible, and spoke out of only one side of his mouth.

"It's about time you got back," he said.

"Why is there only half of you?" Billy asked.

"I'm pretty sure it's these paint fumes. I know you think that all I have to do is whistle 'I've Been Working on the Railroad' and I materialize. But it's not that easy. It takes concentration, and I really think these fumes are interfering with my ability to focus."

"Well, it's highly weird looking at only half of you."

"Hey, half of me is better than the whole of most people."

"If you do say so yourself."

"I just did. So what's the big surprise?"

"You're going to thank me, Hoove, for what I am about to do for you. I have a plan that is not only going to get you ungrounded, but could just get you an A in Responsibility to Others."

"I could use an A. Spill it, Shorty. Whatcha got?"

"This," Billy answered, reaching into the tank and gently lifting Berko out of it. He put the little gecko in the palm of his hand and started across the room so the Hoove could get a clear look. When he got to the windowsill, he held his hand right up to the Hoove's face. He wanted to get close because he wasn't sure if having only one eye visible meant that the Hoove could only see half a gecko.

Instantaneously, the other half of the Hoove appeared, and the look of sheer horror on his face said it all. Screaming, the Hoove zoomed off the windowsill and rocketed across the room, zipping right through the closet door. Billy and Berko swiveled their heads in unison.

"Get that thing away from me!" the Hoove yelled from the closet. His muffled voice sounded more scared than Billy had ever heard it before.

"It's just a little gecko," Billy called. "I got it for you to take care of. To show the Higher-Ups that you can put someone else's needs before yours."

"I'm not taking care of that thing. Not today. Not tomorrow. Not ever."

"What's your problem?"

"My problem is that I'm allergic to lizards."

"You mean they make you itch or give you red bumpy things on your upper arms?"

"No. It means I dislike them intensely."

"Come on out, Hoove. This is Berko. You'll like him."

"Is he a lizard?"

"Yes."

"Then, I don't like him. And I never will. As long as he's out there, I'm staying in here."

Billy felt frustration rising in his voice, but he tried to remain calm. He knew that if he exploded at the Hoove, his plan would fail completely. He tried to take the logical route.

"Listen, Hoove. There is nothing scary about this gecko. He gets along well with others, he's a good sleeper, and enjoys an occasional cricket."

"That's it," the Hoove shouted from the closet. "Not another word, especially about chewable crickets. Thank him very much for coming, he was a real sport about it. And give him my very best wishes as he goes back to whatever cave he crawled out of."

Billy looked down at Berko, who seemed so sweet and innocent. The poor little guy had no idea what had just happened. And Billy had no idea how he was going to explain to Daisy that he wasn't going to be able to keep Berko.

"Hoove, I really think you should get to know him," Billy coaxed. "He has very soulful eyes."

Without waiting for an answer, Billy opened the closet door and found the Hoove tucked inside the pocket of his navy blue winter parka. Only his head and one arm were hanging out — the rest of him was snuggled neatly inside.

"Here," Billy said, thrusting Berko in front of the Hoove's startled eyes. "I dare you to look at him and tell me you don't love him."

Berko stared up at the Hoove and flicked his tongue out in a friendly gesture. A look of total disgust flashed across the Hoove's face, and suddenly, a tangy orange smell filled the closet. Berko's nostrils flared as he took in the scent. He must have liked it because instantly he squirmed out of Billy's hand and sprang over to the parka, landing right next to the pocket that held the Hoove. Billy tried to grab him, but Berko was too fast. He scurried up the fabric, climbed over the edge, and disappeared into the depths of the pocket.

"Yowee kazowee!" the Hoove bellowed. "This lizard is setting up camp in my underwear! Either he goes or I go."

"Get back here right now, Berko," Billy called. "This is no way to make a good first impression!"

"First impression, second impression, last impression," the Hoove said. "There is no good impression. That is final. I have spoken."

And with that, he zoomed out of the parka pocket and took off across the room, flapping his arms and legs as if the little lizard was still attached to him. He was in full-fledged panic mode.

Billy knew that he had lost the argument. There was no doubt that the Hoove was permanently finished with the gecko conversation and had nothing more to contribute other than flapping limbs and a sour orange smell that filled the room with tangy displeasure.

CHAPTER 6

With great sadness, Billy reached into the pocket, found Berko, and placed him back into his little tank. He hated the idea of taking him back to Daisy's, but he could see no other alternative. The Hoove was hovering in the corner of the room giving off nasty fumes and shouting, "This is a gecko-free zone! This is a gecko-free zone!"

"Okay, okay," Billy said as he headed out the door. "I heard you the first time."

He left the house and walked down the front path, where he was stopped by another member of the Brownstone family, Rod the Clod, who was wheeling his bike into their garage.

"What are you carrying there, Broccoli?" Rod said in his usual snarky tone of voice. "Your knitting?"

"Actually, Rod, it's none of your business."

"Everything in this neighborhood is my business. I observe, take notes, and I report unusual events to the proper authorities. As a matter of fact, I just reported Mrs. Pearson because one tire of her electric lawn mower was on the sidewalk."

"You're kidding, right?"

"The sidewalk is public property, Broccoli, and we all have to protect it."

"But Mrs. Pearson is such a nice person. She keeps Hershey Kisses in her pocket for all the kids in the neighborhood."

"Yeah, and most of the time they're melted. Besides, the law doesn't recognize Hershey's Kisses. The law is the law, and if you break even the tiniest fraction of it, the entire neighborhood will crumble. So like I was saying, what do you have in that box?"

"It's not a box, it's a tank," Billy said, turning it around so Rod could see into it. "It happens to contain a fat-tailed African gecko that was my pet for the last seven and a half minutes."

Berko scurried right up to the glass pane and stared at Brownstone, who dropped his bike and backed up so fast his sneakers practically left skid marks on the cement. He tried to contain the scream that was living right at the back of his throat, so the noise that came out of his mouth sounded like a sorry little whimper that even a four-year-old wouldn't make.

"What's your problem, Brownstone?" Billy asked. "You afraid of a little gecko? They don't even have teeth. What do you think, he's going to gum you to death?"

"I'm not afraid of anything," Rod snapped. "I'm on the football team. I knock down guys twice my size. I look fear right in the eyes and say, 'Rod Brownstone is coming for you.'"

"Well, then, come say hello to Berko."

Brownstone shifted uncomfortably. The last thing he wanted to do was let Billy Broccoli see any weakness in him. Puffing up his chest and trying to look as casual as possible, he sauntered very slowly in the direction of the lizard tank. When Berko saw him, the little gecko flicked out his tongue in his usual friendly gesture.

"Eeeekkk!" Rod screamed before he could stop himself. "That thing is vicious." He waved his hands so wildly in the air that he knocked the tank out of Billy's hands and it tumbled onto the lawn. The screen covering the top flew off, and before Billy could put it back on, Berko scurried out and disappeared into the grass.

"Now look what you've done, Brownstone," he shouted, dropping to his knees and crawling around on all fours in the grass. "Don't just stand there. You can at least help me find him. I have to return him to the pet store."

"That thing was ready to attack," Brownstone said. "You better find him and get him off my property or I'm calling the police!"

"What? To file a missing gecko report?"

"No, to alert the authorities that a menace is on the loose. He could be terrorizing an innocent victim at this very moment."

Billy heard a rustling in the hedge nearby.

"Berko, is that you, fella?" he called softly. "Don't be scared. I'm coming for you." Billy dropped to his knees and parted the bushes with his hand, but what he saw lurking inside was in no way a gecko. It was a fat gray-and-white cat slinking around in the shade of the leaves. The cat looked at him and hissed in a definitely unfriendly way.

"Hey, Brownstone," Billy said. "Do cats eat geckos?"

"How should I know?" Brownstone answered. "But I'll tell you one thing. That cat will eat anything. It's always wandering around here looking for food. I should have it arrested for loitering."

Billy looked closely at the cat, trying to determine if it had eaten Berko. It did seem awfully fat around the middle, but at least he wasn't licking his chops as if he had just finished a meal.

"You better not have hurt him," Billy said. The cat just looked at him in a suspicious way and pawed at the air, as if understanding that Billy was making a terrible accusation. There was a long silence as Billy pondered the awful possibility. He felt his stomach flip.

"Hi, guys," came a sweet voice from behind them. Billy was so startled, he whirled around and lost his balance, landing face-first in the grass. It was Ruby Baker walking with her sister, Sophia, to Billy's house for band practice. Sophia was the bass player in Breeze's band, and sometimes Ruby came along to hang out at their rehearsals. Ruby was the most popular girl in the sixth grade, and both Billy and Rod secretly had a crush on her. But Ruby was unaware of their admiring gazes, because she was looking in the palm of her hand.

"Look what I just found," she said.

Billy glanced at her cupped hand ... which held none other than the escaped Berko.

"You found him!" Billy cried, relief filling his body. He jumped up to his feet as fast as he could.

"Yeah, you did," Rod said weakly, dropping to his knees out of fear.

"What are you doing on your knees?" Ruby asked him.

"Tying my shoelaces," he answered far too quickly.

"But they're already tied."

"I'm just making sure that the knot is as tight as possible. You can't be too careful."

"Listen, kids," Sophia said. "Not to interrupt your fascinating shoelace conversation, but I'll see you inside. I have bigger emotional issues to explore than double knots. Breeze and I are writing a new song today about treading water in the dark river of love."

As Sophia headed inside, Billy grabbed the gecko tank from the lawn and took it over to Ruby.

"You are a lifesaver," he said. "Or I should say a gecko-saver. For a minute, I thought a cat had eaten him."

"Oh, that would have been horrible!"

"I know. I'm so happy to see you, Berko."

"Oh, what a cute name." Ruby giggled. "I had a gecko once. Her name was Harmony."

"Did she dine on crickets like Berko does?"

"Totally. Harmony was a real chowhound. I mean, she'd gobble up three crickets a week. I had to put her on a diet because she started looking like a mini Chihuahua."

Feeling left out of the conversation, Rod jumped in with a major fib.

"Yeah, well I had a gecko, too," he said. "And mine ate four crickets a week. He looked like a mini pit bull."

"Oh really?" Ruby said while she gently stroked Berko on his head with her index finger. "What was his name?"

"Uh . . ." Rod stammered. "Uh . . . he was so tough, he didn't need a name. I just called him Him."

Billy knew Rod made up that story just to impress Ruby. No one would ever be that afraid of lizards and geckos if they had actually had one. He couldn't resist the urge to show Rod up for the phony he was.

"Why don't you come over and give Berko a pet or two? I'm sure he would like to say good-bye to you before he goes back to the pet store."

Ruby put her hand out to Rod.

"You can even hold him, if you want."

When Brownstone saw Ruby and Berko coming toward him, he turned a sickly shade of green. Billy thought he saw a few beads of per-spiration break out on the tip of his nose.

"Hey, I'd love to hold him, really." Rod gulped. "I'm a big lizard lover at heart. But I hear my mom calling. And you don't know my mom, but she's got a temper that goes off like a volcano. I've got to go before she erupts."

And turning on his cowardly heels, Rod bar-reled across the lawn and flew into the safety of his house.

"Something tells me he's scared of this harmless little guy," Ruby said.

"Maybe he's not as tough as he pretends to be," Billy said.

Ruby shrugged.

"Boys are so strange," she said to Berko. "But not you. You're a little cutie."

Billy held the tank up to her, and she gently placed Berko back inside. He must have liked being in there because he scurried happily into the safety of his plastic cave.

"He's probably thinking about how strange all us humans are," Billy said. "I bet he'll be glad to get back to his animal friends at the pet shop."

"Why are you taking him back?" Ruby asked.

"He didn't exactly get along with my family."

Ruby nodded. "I can see that," she said. "Breeze doesn't seem like the type of girl who'd relate to any creature who doesn't wear sequined boots."

"Hey," Billy said. "Do you want to come with me to the pet store?"

Suddenly, when he realized that he had actually asked Ruby to come along, his face turned bright red. "I mean, you probably don't want to come," he added quickly, "but if you do, you can. Come along, I mean."

"Sure," Ruby said with a laugh. "It's better than falling into the dark river of love. Can I carry Berko?"

"No problem," Billy answered, handing her the tank. "He really likes you."

It was a ten minute walk to Fur 'N Feathers, but to Billy, it seemed like it only took thirty seconds. Ruby was so easy to talk to. She chatted about her cross-country meets, about their English teacher, Mr. Wallwetter, and how she thought his thin little mustache looked like a plucked eyebrow on his upper lip. Everything she said made Billy laugh. Billy told Ruby about Daisy and her pet parrot, Robert, who liked to croon songs they played on oldies radio stations. Ruby couldn't wait to meet them both.

When they reached Fur 'N Feathers, Daisy was busy feeding alfalfa to the bunnies, gerbils, and hamsters. Robert announced their arrival.

"Crab cakes!" he squawked.

Daisy looked over to the door and broke into a huge smile when she saw Billy and Ruby.

"Oh, don't mind Robert," she said. "He always calls customers he likes crab cakes. I think it's because I got him from Frankie's Fried Fish Stand, where he lived for ten years. If he doesn't like you, he'll call you an oyster. And if he can't stand you, you're tartar sauce . . . and you better watch out!"

As she clomped over to them in her shiny red clogs, Daisy noticed the gecko tank.

"Berko!" she said. "Did you come back for a visit because you missed us? What a sweet gecko you are!"

"Actually, Daisy, I have a slight problem I need to discuss with you," Billy began sheepishly.

"Oh," she said in a hushed voice. "Was it something he ate? He tends to battle diarrhea."

"No, his stomach was fine. At least from what I could see. The problem is that I can't keep him."

"Oh," Daisy said. "Didn't your friend like him?"

Billy glanced at Ruby, who had a confused look on her face. He motioned to Daisy to follow him down the aisle toward the gerbil section so that they could have a little privacy.

"That's Ruby over there," he whispered. "And she doesn't know about my friend, so can we keep that part between us?"

"Oh." Daisy smiled. "You have two girl-friends. You little Romeo, you."

"No, no, it's nothing like that. I just like to keep my pet interactions private. So can we keep this quiet?"

"I get it," Daisy said with a wink. "Mum's the word."

Ruby had taken Berko over to visit Robert and was having a fine time with both animals. Berko sat at the edge of his tank, flicking his tongue up at Robert as if to say, "Nice to see you again, old pal." When Daisy and Billy joined her, Ruby was laughing with the animals like they were old friends.

"Are you sure you have to give Berko back?" she said to Billy. "He's really got a lot of personality."

"The thing I've learned, honey," Daisy said, taking Berko's tank from Ruby's hands, "is that all members of a family have to enjoy the pet or it just won't work. So if Berko isn't loved by everyone at Billy's house, then perhaps it's not the right home for him."

"That makes sense," Ruby agreed. "I had to give Harmony away because the crickets we fed her interfered with my sister's creative process. She's a bass guitar player and the crickets always chirped off the beat."

Daisy took Berko to the reptile aisle and placed him back in his original glass tank next to Bruce the tarantula.

"I was hoping I could exchange him for another pet," Billy said. "Something really low maintenance."

"Well," Daisy said, "the only thing lower maintenance than Berko would be a fish. Let me show you three or four kinds of fish so you can make a decision."

One whole wall of Fur 'N Feathers was devoted to the aquariums. Some held iridescent neon tetras, some had exotic tropical fish like angelfish and clown fish. One tank was divided into two separate compartments, each one holding only one fish: a bluish-white one and an orange one. They seemed to be staring at each other through the glass in a very unfriendly way.

"I know what those are," Ruby said. "They're Siamese fighting fish. If you put them in the same tank, they'll fight to the death."

A fighting fish sounded like it had a lot of spunk in it, and Billy thought Hoover would like that. The Hoove prided himself on his spunk, so it seemed like the perfect match. Besides, Billy could only buy one, which meant that it wouldn't be a lot of work to take care of. Drop a few fish flakes in there every day, change the water occasionally. Even an irresponsible guy like the Hoove could manage that. It sounded to Billy like an easy A in Responsibility to Others.

"I think I'd like the orange Siamese fighting fish," he told Daisy. "He seems really cool."

"I could exchange that fish for Berko," Daisy said, "and you'd still have a little money left over to buy some food. These fish eat a special kind of flake made from bloodworms and mashed shrimp."

"Sounds delicious," Ruby laughed. "Remind me to sprinkle some on my cereal."

"Siamese fighting fish like to stare through the bowl and watch humans going about their business," Daisy said. "It's very stimulating to them. So this fish will need company."

"Oh, no problem there," Billy said. "My friend . . . I mean my family . . . will haunt him night and day. You can be sure of that."

"Then he's yours!" Daisy said. "I'll get him ready for the trip home."

"Thank you so much, Daisy," Billy said, "for everything you've done for me. By the way, does my new fish have a name?"

Daisy shook her head.

"Good. I think I'm going to call him Kung Fu. Because he's a fighter."

"That's perfect," Ruby said. "I love kung fu movies."

While Daisy scooped Kung Fu out of the aquarium and placed him in a plastic bag filled with the water he just came out of, Ruby went over to Robert's perch and tried to teach him a new Beyoncé song.

"Come on, buddy," she said to him. "You've got to get a little more current with your musical tastes."

But poor Robert just couldn't shake his tail feathers.

As for Billy, his mind was racing with excitement about finally having a solution to the Hoove's problem. Every bit of logic told him that Kung Fu and the Hoove were a perfect match.

Which just goes to prove that logic isn't always right.

CHAPTER 7

When Billy and Ruby got home, Sophia was waiting on the front lawn. And she was fuming mad.

"Where have you been?" she asked Ruby. "Our rehearsal ended ten minutes ago and mom's been calling constantly. She needs us to give the dog a tomato juice bath because he got sprayed by a skunk again and the whole house reeks."

"That crazy Buster," Ruby said with a laugh. "He never learns. He keeps chasing skunks and they blast him every time."

"You won't be laughing fifteen minutes from now when your nose is filled with skunk stink." Sophia started down the sidewalk. "Come on, Ruby. I'm not going to wash that mutt by myself."

Ruby said good-bye to Billy and Kung Fu.

"Call me later and let me know how Mr. Fu is doing," she said to Billy. He couldn't believe his ears.

"You want *me* to call you?" It was the first time any girl had ever suggested that. "Sure I'll call. Sure. Sure. Sure." He didn't mean to say *sure* three times, but somehow the words tumbled out of his mouth all by themselves. He heard his voice getting higher with each *sure*, so by the third one, he sounded like a squeaky mouse.

After watching Ruby and Sophia disappear down the block, Billy walked up the flagstone path to the front door. He couldn't reach into his pocket for his key and hold on to the plastic bag while balancing the fishbowl and mini net he got from Daisy, so he turned his back to the door and knocked with the heel of his shoe.

"Somebody open the door," he called out.

"Open it yourself," came Breeze's voice from inside.

"I would if I could, but I can't so I won't," he yelled back.

"You are such a helpless toad," Breeze shouted.

"Hey!" Rod's voice boomed from next door. "Can you turkeys keep it down out there? Some people are trying to watch cartoons in here."

"Mind your own business, Brownstone," Billy and Breeze yelled in unison. They could fight all they wanted between themselves, but when it came to Rod Brownstone calling them names, they were a team. No matter how much Breeze admired Rod Brownstone's big muscles, she didn't admire his big mouth. Billy gave one more kick on the door with his heel, and this time, it opened. But it wasn't Breeze standing there. In fact, no one was there except a detached hand floating on the doorknob.

"What's with the hand only, Hoove? Haven't you gotten control of your invisibility yet?"

"Hey, don't give me a hard time. The door is open, right?"

Billy walked past the Hoove's hand and said, "Come with me. I have something for you."

"It better not have a forked tongue."

Billy hurried into his bedroom before the Hoove could get a good look at Kung Fu.

By the time Hoover floated down the hall and reached Billy's room, he had grown two legs and a neck. He was forty-seven percent there.

"You know, if I didn't know you better, you'd

terrify me," Billy said. "You have to admit it's creepy seeing a floating neck with no head."

"Don't say another word for the next two minutes," the Hoove answered. "I'm going to focus my majestic powers of concentration and produce the rest of my body. Trust me, just being a neck is not my idea of a party."

While the Hoove took himself into the corner to concentrate, Billy went into the bathroom and filled the fishbowl with water. Returning to his room, he submerged the plastic bag in the bowl, so that Kung Fu would adapt to the temperature of the new water. After a few minutes, Billy opened the plastic bag and released Kung Fu into his new home. The fish spread his fins and swam around the bowl, defiantly nipping at the glass.

"There you go, boy," Billy said. "That's the way to strut your stuff."

"Thank you. Stuff strutting is my calling card," the Hoove answered, thinking Billy was talking to him. "You say Hoover Porterhouse, and people say, there's his stuff being strut."

Hoover's powers of concentration must have worked because when he floated over to Billy, his whole body had materialized, except for his left ear, which always proved to be a problem.

"I wasn't talking to you," Billy said to him. "I was talking to Kung Fu. Your new fish friend. Here to help you demonstrate to the Higher-Ups that you are more responsible than a troop of Girl Scouts."

"Got to give you credit, Billy Boy. You're a determined little go-getter." The Hoove peeked around Billy to get a look at the fishbowl. "Okay, let's take a gander at your second colossal failure."

Billy held up the bowl, and the Hoove stared at Kung Fu, who by now had flared his colorful orange fins so wide that he appeared twice his size. The Hoove circled the bowl, checking out the fish from every angle.

"Now this is a pet worthy of the Hoove," he said.

"He's a Siamese fighting fish," Billy said. "Daisy at the pet store told me that in Thailand, they call them *ikan bettah*, which means 'biting fish.'"

"I like it," the Hoove said as he started

karate chopping the air. "I like it a lot. What's he got in that mouth of his? Fangs?"

"Now you sound like Bennett," Billy said, "wanting to check out everyone's dental situation. I don't know what he's got in there. I haven't pried his mouth open."

The Hoove pressed his face up to the glass and studied Kung Fu carefully. At first, the fish stayed completely still, as if he was sizing up his enemy. Each time the Hoove moved, Kung Fu's eyes followed him with a laserlike stare. When the Hoove put his hand on the rim of the bowl, Kung Fu took a fighting stance, shooting out his fins to their full extent and letting them ripple in the water as if he were flexing his muscles.

"Hey, we're a lot alike, you and me," the Hoove said. "We're tough and extremely good-looking."

Billy was relieved to see that the Hoove had taken an immediate liking to Kung Fu. He seized the opportunity to educate him about everything he'd have to do to take good care of him.

"He doesn't require much maintenance," Billy began, "which I think is a great place for you to start. I got some mashed-shrimp-and-bloodworm flakes from the pet store, and you just have to drop a few into his bowl every day."

"That's certainly better than handling a cricket," the Hoove said, nodding.

"And of course you have to clean his bowl and change the water once a week."

"Change the water? You mean after he pee pees in it? That part is not so appealing. Maybe I can hire your mother to do it for me."

"That's exactly the point, Hoove. Being responsible means taking care of things yourself, not putting them off on other people. You have to clean the bowl and change the water yourself. Now, I know you don't like that idea, but if you think about it, it's not much of a sacrifice to make in exchange for your freedom, is it?"

"Okay, but I've got to wear rubber gloves."

"On what, exactly? You don't have hands!"

"What are you, the official hand monitor?"

Billy didn't answer. Now that the Hoove was showing interest in taking care of a pet, he wanted to keep the mood light and friendly.

He was taking no chances on setting off the Hoove's hot temper.

"Hey, we need to give Fuey here a welcome party," the Hoove was saying. "Give me a couple of those fish flakes. I'm going to give them to him personally."

Billy handed the Hoove the cylinder of fish flakes. The lid was sealed tight, and in an effort to pull it open, the Hoove dropped the container, and the flakes spilled all over the rug. He bent down and picked up a pinch of them.

"Wait. You're going to give him food from the floor?" Billy objected.

"First of all, he's a fish, he's not going to notice. And second of all, the way your mother keeps this house clean, *you* could eat off the floor."

The Hoove dropped a few of the flakes into the bowl and watched them float on top of the water. Kung Fu circled the biggest flake, and then suddenly attacked it, snapping it from the surface.

"Don't you just love the way he moves through the water?" the Hoove said. "Sleek like a speeding motorcycle. I've got to try that."

And before Billy could utter a sound, the Hoove turned to smoke and dove into the fishbowl like it was his personal swimming pool. Immediately, he shrunk to the size of a goldfish, doing the breaststroke around the bowl with his dark hair streaming out around him like thousands of tiny wiggling worms. With a powerful dolphin kick, he somersaulted right up to Kung Fu's startled face and blew a steady stream of bubbles at him, as if to say, "Hey, pal, you want to play?" But Kung Fu, unlike his name, was no fighter. He took one look at the transparent, ghostly face in front of him, and using the full force of his elongated fins, propelled himself straight up into the air and out of the bowl. He hung there in space for a split second, which seemed like an eternity to an amazed Billy. Then, without further ado, Kung Fu fell through the air and landed in a belly flop on the rug. Billy gasped.

The Hoove poked his head out of the glass fishbowl.

"Hey, where do you think you're going?" he called out. "Come back here, little fishy. I'm here to take care of you!"

"You're not taking care of him!" Billy screamed. "You're scaring the pants off him!"

"Well, excuse me. I didn't notice he was wearing pants."

There was no time for Billy to explain that it was just an expression. A petrified Kung Fu was dragging his fishy body across the rug as fast as his fins could take him. He was heading for the door, undoubtedly trying to get back to the unhaunted safety of Daisy's store.

The Hoove spun out of the bowl and hovered in the air. "Come back here," he called to Kung Fu. "Once you get to know me, I'm going to knock your socks off."

Kung Fu turned his head in the direction of the Hoove's voice, and glanced back at him.

"That's right! Come to Papa." The Hoove smiled. "I've got some yummy bloodworms right here."

Kung Fu's eyes bulged, and he scooted toward the door like his life depended on it.

"I have to rescue him," Billy said, grabbing the mini net Daisy had given him.

"Give me that," the Hoove said, reaching for the net. "I'll do it."

"You can't! He's terrified of you, Hoove! Don't even think about going near him."

"I thought you said he was my pet. I'm supposed to take care of him. If he just gives me a chance, we'll be pals."

There was no time for any more discussion. Kung Fu had been out of the water too long. His fins were growing limp, and he needed to get back in the bowl so he could breathe again. Billy grabbed the net in his right hand and, lunging forward, scooped Kung Fu off the carpet. Pivoting like a basketball player, he skyhooked the little fish into the bowl just in the nick of time. Kung Fu sank to the bottom while both Billy and the Hoove held their breath, hoping he would be okay.

After about ten seconds, his orange fins started to spread out and Kung Fu balanced himself on his tail. From the bottom of the bowl, he stared up at Billy, as if to say, "Can somebody please get me out of here?" He looked miserable.

The Hoove, relieved that his pet was seemingly back to normal, pressed his face up against the bowl and saw the same expression Billy did.

"That is one unhappy fish," he said. "Look at him. He's giving me the stink eye."

"I don't think he's ever been around a ghost before, Hoove. I'm sure it's nothing personal."

"Do you think if we give him time, I'll grow on him?" the Hoove asked softly.

The answer was clear. As soon as Kung Fu saw the Hoove's face, he immediately darted to the other side of the bowl and cowered as far away from the Hoove as he could get.

"You know what, Hoove," Billy said. "Maybe it's not going to work out between you and Kung Fu."

The Hoove was silent, and for the first time, Billy actually felt sorry for him.

"But don't worry," Billy continued, trying to make his voice sound bright and peppy. "We'll find the right pet for you. I'm not going to give up."

Billy picked up the bowl and headed for the door. The Hoove hovered quietly in the hallway, trying to assume a casual air. He was sad to see Kung Fu go, but in his usual fashion, he wasn't about to show it.

"Hey, take care, Fuey. Even if you don't like my style, I like yours. Give my regards to all the lady fish at the shop."

He laughed as Billy headed for the front door, but Billy could tell it was a forced laugh, the kind the Hoove used to cover up hurt feelings.

Billy couldn't blame him. It was tough being rejected by a Siamese fighting fish. With a deep sigh of frustration mixed with a little sadness, Billy left the house and headed to Daisy's shop for the last time.

CHAPTER 8

When Billy got home from Daisy's Fur 'N Feathers shop, he was petless and idealess. His once great plan for helping the Hoove by getting him an animal to take care of and learn from had fizzled out like three-day-old ginger ale.

"What's wrong, honey?" his mom asked as he walked in the kitchen door. "You look so dejected."

"I can't seem to figure out how to help a friend of mine."

"Why don't you invite him over for dinner? We're having spicy meatballs with red mushroom sauce. That cheers everyone up."

"Almost everyone. Spicy meatballs give him gas."

Breeze, who was sitting at the kitchen table doing her homework, looked up and made a gagging sound. "Just tell this gas tank, whoever he is, not to come within one hundred yards of this house. You boys and your gas obsession. It's disgusting."

"I'm going to my bedroom until dinner," Billy said, heading out of the kitchen. "I don't need to stay here and have the digestion of my entire gender criticized."

"Now that you have fresh new paint on your walls," Billy's mom called after him, "this would be a good time to get your things organized. Oh, and by the way, do you know someone named Hoover?"

Billy stopped dead in his tracks.

"Why do you ask?"

"I found this envelope on the back porch. It's addressed to someone named Hoover."

"That's for me," Billy said, running to the counter and snatching the envelope. "It's my new nickname. Some of the guys on the baseball team call me that."

"Why?"

"Uh . . . because it rhymes with . . . uh . . . mover. Yeah, that's it. Hoover the Mover."

Breeze gave Billy a suspicious look. "Call me crazy," she said, "but of all the words to describe you, *mover* would be, like, last on my list."

"Well I have many sides that you don't have a clue about," Billy said. "Live and learn."

Before any more questions could arise, he galloped down the hall to his bedroom. He found the Hoove in his closet, lying on his back on the top shelf where Billy kept his sweatshirts and sweaters.

"Don't you knock before entering somebody's personal space?" the Hoove said without even glancing over at Billy.

"I know you're feeling bad about Kung Fu," Billy said. "But if it's any consolation, that fish turned out to be a major mama's boy. He only perked up when he saw Daisy. Some fighting fish he is. All show and no bite."

"Yeah. He's got the look, but he doesn't walk the walk. Or maybe I should say 'swim the swim . . . fin the fin.'"

"I get it, I get it. Oh, by the way, a letter came for you," Billy said, handing the envelope over. The Hoove ripped it open and orange sparks flew from it, shooting up to the ceiling like fireworks with such force that the blast blew the Hoove right out of the closet and into the middle of the room. When the smoke cleared, the Hoove and Billy stood there amazed as a huge can of soup the size of a large-screen television materialized in the air.

"Do the Higher-Ups live in a soup can?" Billy asked.

"They live wherever they want to live."

With a loud creek, the top of the soup can opened and letters started to flow out.

"Look, it's alphabet soup," Billy said, actually rather thrilled because that was his favorite kind of soup.

"Don't get so tickled, Billy Boy. I have a feeling it's not such good news. Look what it says."

The letters had plastered themselves on the wall of Billy's room, spelling out the words *PROGRESS REPORT* in large, doughy noodle shapes, with an occasional carrot or chunk of potato for emphasis.

"Don't be negative," Billy told the Hoove. "Maybe it's going to say you're doing better."

"No, good news comes in cream puffs or French fries." The Hoove shook his head and sighed. "Canned soup means you messed up. Every ghost knows that."

A small flash of light flickered, and soon, five words written in those same noodle letters appeared: *NO SIGNIFICANT PROGRESS. STILL GROUNDED!* They were followed by an exclamation mark made from what appeared to be a mixture of overcooked green beans and celery. As quickly as they had formed, they disappeared from the wall.

The Hoove slumped down on the ground, obviously very disappointed. Billy felt bad for him.

"Come on, Hoove," he said. "Let's talk this through. There has to be a way to get you ungrounded. Maybe the pet thing isn't the way to go."

The Hoove floated out of the closet and over to Billy's desk, perching himself on the edge of the open top drawer.

"To tell you the truth," he sighed, "I was never much of a hit with the animal kingdom. The horses on our ranchero would never let me ride them. In fact, a brown-and-white-spotted mare named Pinto Bean once had the nerve to throw me on the ground right outside this window. All I did was say 'giddy-up, Gasbag.'"

"There was a stable here?"

"Sure. The barn was where the Brownstone house is now. Matter of fact, it's still a barn when you consider that Rod the Cow lives there."

"You must have gotten along with some of the animals," Billy said. "After all, you lived right here on the same property with them. Didn't you have a prize pig that won a ribbon at the county fair or something?"

"You've been reading too many children's books, Billy Boy. It wasn't like that at all. Most of the animals would just skedaddle when I showed up. Except for Penelope. She was a real sweetheart. She loved to nuzzle."

"Penelope?"

"A goat. We were buddies. I'd feed her a handful of alfalfa, and she'd nuzzle my neck. The little beard under her chin tickled, but I got used it."

"So you took care of her?" Billy asked, his mind starting to race with possibilities.

"Yeah. Fed her. Milked her. She followed me everywhere I went. Whenever folks saw me, they knew Penelope couldn't be far behind. It was a sad day when they took her away."

"What happened?"

"Her appetite got out of hand. She'd eat anything — laundry off the line, leather shoes, the carrots from the vegetable garden. But when she chowed down on my mother's best dress and left only a zipper and a pile of neatly stacked buttons, that was the end of Penelope."

"They killed her?"

"Again, my friend, you've been reading too many books. They gave her away to a grapefruit farm in the Imperial Valley, where we were told she developed a great taste for citrus. Man, oh man, I was heartbroken when she left. Never even got a chance to say good-bye. One day she was my best friend, the next day she was nowhere to be seen."

"Hoove, will you excuse me?" Billy said.

"What'd you do, burp? I thought I smelled asparagus."

"No, I mean excuse me from the room."

"Was it something I said?"

"I just have to look something up on the computer. A homework assignment I just remembered. I'll be back soon."

Billy charged down the hall and into the kitchen. Breeze was sitting at the family computer, which they kept on a little desk in the kitchen nook.

"I have to get on the computer," Billy said urgently.

Breeze ignored him.

"I mean it, Breeze. This is really important. I'll just use it for forty-five seconds, then give it right back."

"That's not happening, Billy. I'm right in the middle of something more important."

"Oh really? I didn't know tweeting about your new hair color was that monumental."

"That's because your hair is the color of mud."

"Kids, stop this bickering," Mrs. Broccoli-Fielding said. "Breeze, Billy's only asking for forty-five seconds. Why don't you let him get what he needs done, then you'll have the computer back in a jiffy. Besides, you can use the time to help me set the table."

Breeze gave Billy a look that would refreeze a melting iceberg.

"Thanks a lot, creep," she whispered as she clicked the screen closed. "Look what you started. Next week, you set the table every night. And clear, too."

Billy sat down at the computer and Googled the word *goat*. A million entries came up, from a YouTube video of fainting goats to a restaurant in Kalamazoo, Michigan, called Goat to a chart with instructions on how to breed goats. As he scanned the long list, his eye fell on just the thing he was looking for. He couldn't believe his luck.

RENT-A-GOAT LOS ANGELES, it said.

He clicked on it, and the site's home page came up. It showed a picture of a happy-looking goat with a caption that said, "Why Use a Lawn Mower When You Can Use Me?" Billy read on. The site offered goat rental for the purposes of trimming your lawn or clearing your brush or pulling your weeds. It claimed that goats were an environmentally friendly alternative to garden chemicals. Plus, they were an easier way to get the job done than using human labor. Billy grabbed a sticky note from the desk and jotted down the phone number.

"Here, you can have your precious computer back," he said to Breeze. In his hurry to get back to his room to make the call, he forgot to close the screen. When Breeze sat down, she burst out laughing.

"Goats?" she said. "What are you looking up, your ancestors?"

"I can't hear you," Billy called as he hurried down the hall.

"Why, do you have alfalfa in your ears?" Breeze shouted back.

But Billy wasn't in the mood for bickering with his stepsister anymore. He was a man on a mission.

He burst into his room and, without even saying hello to the Hoove, grabbed for his phone and dialed the number he had jotted down on the sticky note.

"Rent-A-Goat," a man's voice said. "Smiley speaking."

"I'd like to inquire about renting a goat," Billy said.

"You tell me what you need it for, I'll get you the perfect goat," Smiley said. "We've got Charmaine, who is great at keeping your grass trimmed. Grady loves brush and thicket. Clem will eat anything, including poison oak and ivy. He's got a stomach like a tank. And Beatrice, who, to be perfectly honest, is a good goat, but you got to constantly watch her because she'd just as soon hang out with humans as do her job."

"I'll take Beatrice," Billy said without a moment of hesitation. "She sounds perfect for what I have in mind. How much would she cost for a weekend?"

"Well, usually it's about twenty-five dollars a day, but I can give you a break on Beatrice. She's a lover, not a worker. Tell you what, you sound like a nice kid. I'll charge you twenty-five bucks for the whole weekend."

"I have to go ask my parents," Billy said. "But I promise, I'll call you right back."

He hung up the phone and did a little happy dance in his room, pretending to be a head-butting goat.

"Hoove!" he called out. "I think I got you a goat!"

The Hoove didn't answer. Billy wasn't sure where he was. But it didn't matter at that moment because Billy was flying high with enthusiasm. He could already visualize the Hoove and Beatrice, nuzzling up a storm. The Higher-Ups would be blown away by his ability to love and nurture and take care of one of nature's creatures. All he had to do was convince the family that this was a good plan.

When Billy entered the kitchen, Bennett had just come home from a hard day of excavating plaque off an assortment of molars and was hanging up his white dental jacket on the coatrack.

"Hello, Bill," he said. "You're looking in fine spirits."

"That's because I have a great idea, Bennett."

"Watch out, Dad," Breeze said. "I have a feeling this is going to involve goats."

"Actually, she's right," Billy said. "We've been studying the environment in school, and ways that we can all engage in earth-friendly practices."

"I'm so glad to see that you're being motivated by that unit," Billy's mom said as she stirred the mushrooms that were browning on the stove. She was the principal of his school and was very eco-friendly. "I fought to put it in the sixth-grade science program."

"And it was a great idea, Mom. What I'm proposing is that we rent a goat — but only for the weekend."

"What'd I tell you?" Breeze sighed. "I saw that one coming from miles away."

"Turns out goats are an excellent, earth-friendly way to mow your lawn and clear unwanted brush," Billy explained. "My plan is to bring in a goat and let it tidy up our backyard. Bennett, you wouldn't have to mow on Sunday. And Mom, a goat could clear that weed patch so you could finally put in the organic vegetable garden you want. All I need from you is twenty-five dollars and I'll do all the rest."

"Goats stink," Breeze said. "And they make pellets. How are you planning to deal with that, youngster?"

"I promise I will take care of everything goat-related," Billy said. "From pellet to smell it."

Bennett looked over at Billy's mom.

"What do you think, Charlotte? Are you in the mood to host a goat this weekend?"

"I think it sounds like an excellent family project," Mrs. Broccoli-Fielding said, nodding approvingly.

"Wait! Do I get a vote in this?" Breeze whined.

"Apparently not, but thanks for asking," Billy answered. Then, turning to his parents, he said, "This is so great, you guys. You won't regret a minute of it. Just leave everything to me."

Billy raced back to his room and called Smiley back.

"We're on," he said. "What's the earliest Beatrice can be here on Saturday?"

"She likes to sleep late," Smiley answered. "But let me see if I can budge the old lazybones by ten. That work for you?"

"We'll be ready. And thank you, sir," Billy said, slamming down the phone with excitement.

"Ready for what?" It was the Hoove, floating in through the window and catching the very end of Billy's phone conversation.

"Where have you been?" Billy asked him. "You missed all the excitement."

"I was going crazy all locked up in here," the Hoove said, "so I tried to go out for a spin, but I couldn't get farther than the shrubs. That stupid invisible wall wouldn't let me through."

"Hoove," Billy said with a smile, "I think I finally found your wall buster. And believe it or not, her name is Beatrice."

CHAPTER 9

Ten o'clock Saturday could not come soon enough for Billy. By that time, the Hoove had driven him officially crazy, floating from room to room and complaining nonstop that he was bored and had nothing to do. He was like a cooped-up lion prowling around the house, his mood growing worse with each passing day. Billy had tried to interest him in getting involved in a craft project like building a LEGO city or painting a model car, the kind of projects his mother always encouraged him to do when he was home sick. But the Hoove laughed at LEGOs and had no patience for that kind of thing.

"Maybe engaging in building plastic castles from little blocks is amusing to the likes of you," he told Billy, "but it definitely does not float my pirate ship, if you get my drift. Hoover

Porterhouse the Third was born to be out and about, to strut my stuff in the public arena."

"But how, Hoove? You're invisible," Billy pointed out.

"And you're annoying," the Hoove snapped.

Being grounded had not helped his disposition one bit. He was as prickly as a cactus and twice as thorny. Billy hoped that the sight of the goat would rekindle the Hoove's warm feelings for Penelope and motivate him to take such good care of Beatrice that he'd really impress the Higher-Ups. He spent hours and hours preparing the Hoove so he'd know just what to do. He checked out a book from the library on goat tending and read it to the Hoove every night. They reviewed what kinds of hay goats like to eat, how to use a goat brush to scratch their backs, even how to trim and polish their hooves. But the question with Hoover Porterhouse was not if he knew *what* to do, but if he was *willing* to do it. He was one stubborn ghost, that was for sure.

By nine o'clock on Saturday morning, Billy was up, showered, and dressed with a clean

T-shirt on and his hair slicked back with some of his sister's mousse.

"May I point out," the Hoove said when Billy emerged from the bathroom all scrubbed and ready, "that we are entertaining a goat, and not a young lady?"

"I want to make a good impression on Beatrice," Billy said. "And you should, too. She's going to have to trust you so she'll let you take care of her for the weekend."

"Well, then, excuse me while I put on my tuxedo and white gloves," the Hoove answered. "I didn't know goats were so fussy about fashion."

"Now remember," Billy said, ignoring the Hoove's sarcasm, "you have to be very responsible while Beatrice is here. Close the gate when she arrives so she doesn't escape. And put down some straw in the garage so she can lie down and relax when she's finished with work. And always keep her water bucket full."

"What am I, a farmhand?"

"You're grounded, that's what you are. And if you want to get ungrounded, this is your chance to strut your stuff, as you would say. So give it all you've got."

"Yeah, yeah, yeah," the Hoove said. Although he sounded bored, Billy felt that he was actually listening to his advice. He was just desperate enough to do what he was told.

When Smiley's truck pulled up, it created quite a stir in the neighborhood. It was a red truck with the words RENT-A-GOAT printed in big white letters along the side. The bed of the truck was filled with hay, and behind that, a horse trailer with a pink canopy was attached. Along the side of the canopy it said, "Call Smiley: He's Sure to Get Your Goat!"

Billy dashed out the front door with Hoover floating right behind him, but before he could reach the truck, he was met by Rod Brownstone storming over to their front lawn, his binoculars draped around his neck. His little sister Amber, still in her bunny-rabbit pajamas, trailed behind.

"What's the big idea?" Rod snarled. "Wild animals aren't allowed in this neighborhood."

"That's a goat, Brownstone," Billy said. "It's not exactly wild."

"Oh yeah, well, you're a goat," Rod snapped back with his usual quick wit.

"I'll handle this," the Hoove said. He zipped up right next to Rod's melon-size head and yanked three times on his fleshy earlobe before sticking his finger into his ear and wiggling it around like a mosquito was buzzing around in there. Then he did the same thing on the other ear.

Rod grabbed his ear, but somehow managed to say, "And you smell like a sack of rotten oranges, too."

Billy had planned this day so that everything would go smoothly. He didn't want any trouble from Rod, so he just ignored his insults.

"That goat is spending the weekend with us," he explained. "Cleaning up the yard. Why don't you come meet her?"

"My brother's afraid of animals," Amber blurted out. "He's a scaredy-cat."

"I am not," Rod snapped.

"Are, too," she answered. "Aren't undercover agents supposed to tell the truth?"

"I would come meet your stupid goat, no problem," Rod said to Billy, "but I'm busy right now. I'm . . . I'm . . . having company and I have to get the house ready."

"Teddy and Jack are coming to play with me, not you," Amber shouted. "They don't care if the house is messy. You're just scared."

Rod gave Amber such a fierce look, she screamed and took off running across the lawn to the house.

"Mommy," she yelled. "Rod's making the mean face at me again!"

"I am not," he yelled, chasing her into the house, which Billy realized gave Rod the perfect excuse to avoid coming anywhere near the goats.

Billy and the Hoove headed for the truck, reaching it just as Smiley was climbing out of the cab. He was a small man in overalls, with light, wide-set eyes and a long white goatee. He actually looked a little like a goat, but without the horns, of course.

"You Billy?" he said. "I hope you're ready. Them goats is kicking up a storm back there."

"Wait a minute," the Hoove said to Billy. "He said goats. I thought we were getting *a* goat, as in one."

"I'll handle this," Billy whispered to him. Then, turning to Smiley, he said politely, "I think we only ordered one goat, sir."

"Yeah, well, Grady wasn't doing anything today, so I thought I'd throw him in for free," Smiley said. "He's a real muncher, not like lazy old Beatrice here."

"Well, I guess that's okay," Billy said. "After all, two goats are better than one."

"Says who?" the Hoove complained. "Two goats take twice as much work, and not to be gross, also make twice as many pellets. Who's going to clean those up? Trust me, not yours truly."

But the Hoove's protests were too late. Smiley had already opened up the back of the horse trailer and was guiding two goats onto the street. They were both sneezing.

"Do your goats have a cold?" Billy asked Smiley.

"Nah, they just sneeze when they're alarmed. All goats do. It'll stop as soon as they get used to you."

He led the goats over to Billy.

"This one's Grady," he said, petting a large brown-and-white goat with a long beard and an impressive set of horns. "And this fatso over here is the one and only Beatrice," he added, pulling on a rope to guide a white goat, who looked like she had a baby goat in her stomach, onto the curb.

Beatrice let out a long bleat that sounded like an unhappy toddler calling her mother.

"Maaaaaaaah," she complained, and Billy couldn't really blame her. No one likes being called a fatso, even a goat. Right away, Billy liked Beatrice, and what was even more surprising was that the Hoove did, too. Beatrice walked up to Billy and put her chin right next to his chest, giving him a thoroughly wonderful nuzzle. The Hoove floated over to her tentatively. He had grown cautious of animals after he was so cruelly rejected by Kung Fu. But unlike Kung Fu, Beatrice didn't seem bothered by his ghostliness at all. She nuzzled the general area of his midsection, or where his midsection would have been, if he had an actual body, the same way Penelope had done back in the old days. She had been such a good goat. He remembered the time he visited her in the barn and brought her an entire sack of turnips. She dug into them like candy while he went to get her fresh water. When he came back with the water, he discovered that she had devoured the whole sack but had saved one purple turnip, which she held between her teeth and dropped at his feet, as if to say, "I saved this one for you." With this memory in his mind and Beatrice nuzzling his body, a huge smile spread across the Hoove's face.

"This goat has excellent taste," he beamed. "Clearly, she knows a quality person when she sees one."

Smiley was a little confused. Since the Hoove was totally invisible to him, what he saw was Beatrice nuzzling air.

"Come on, you crazy old thing," he said, giving her rope a gentle tug. "You're here to work, not to blow kisses in the air." Then, with a laugh, he looked at Billy and said, "Goats, you gotta love 'em."

Smiley and the two goats followed Billy across the front yard and over to the side gate that led to the backyard. Billy noticed Rod peering through his binoculars from his living room window. He had the urge to set one of the goats loose in the Brownstone backyard just to freak Rod out, but thought better of it. That would set a poor example for the Hoove, who had already unlatched the gate and was holding it open.

"Right this way, kids," Hoover told the goats, giving each of them a little bow and a stroke of their heads as they passed. He was really on his best behavior, and a wave of hope swept over Billy. This was the Hoover Porterhouse the Higher-Ups had been waiting to see. At last, they had a plan that was going to work.

When the goats reached the backyard, the whole family was waiting to greet them. Bennett had his camera and started snapping pictures right away. Mrs. Broccoli-Fielding fed each of them a granola bar as a welcome treat. Even Breeze had graced the scene with her presence, although she had put on some heavy work boots with her shorts to make sure her feet didn't come into contact with any stray pellets.

While Billy's parents signed some paper-work and gave Smiley his money, the Hoove got busy helping Grady and Beatrice get adjusted. He and Billy walked them toward the back of the yard, where the grass was tallest and the garden least tended. Grady headed right for a stack of dandelion weeds that had been pulled up, but not thrown away yet, and dug in like it was a T-bone steak. Beatrice hung out next to the Hoove, taking a bite or two of grass and then nuzzling him while she chewed. And chewed. And chewed. Goats have four stomachs, so there was a lot of chewing involved.

Billy worried that Beatrice and Grady would be upset when Smiley left. But after the bill was settled, Smiley just gave each goat a gentle swat on the rump and said, "See you tomorrow, you old goats," and left. Grady and Beatrice didn't even bleat good-bye. They just snuggled up to the Hoove like he was their long lost dad.

For the first hour, the two goats cruised around the backyard, taking bites of grass and weeds and ivy with an occasional piece of cardboard or a leftover seed packet thrown in. The Hoove was gentle as could be, brushing stray twigs off their beards, leading them to a couple of avocados that had fallen off the tree, helping scratch their backs when they rubbed up against the tree trunks. At one point, Billy saw him staring at a little sparrow sitting on a low branch of the peach tree.

"See that bird?" the Hoove said to Billy. "He used to be a bald eagle. He works for the Higher-Ups. I think they sent him here to check on me."

Billy didn't want to start up a conversation with the Hoove with his family nearby, so he didn't answer, just nodded.

"Why don't you go tell your bosses how good I'm doing," the Hoove yelled at the bird. "Tell them I am the picture of responsibility. Tell them I am Mr. Responsibility himself. Go on, make yourself useful for once!"

"You should talk," the bird chirped. "I wouldn't call babysitting a couple of bearded cows exactly useful."

"They're goats," the Hoove snapped. "I'd think you'd know that."

"Goats, cows. They're all just four-legged poopers in need of scoopers to me."

Billy was very surprised when the bird spoke, then took off and flew high in the sky, disappearing at lightning speed. It seemed unbelievable to him that the sparrow worked for the Higher-Ups, but ever since he had met Hoover Porterhouse, he had learned that many things that seemed unbelievable were actually true.

It didn't take long for Breeze to get bored.

"I'm going inside." She yawned. "All this chomping is getting on my nerves."

Gradually, Billy's parents drifted away, too. When you get right down to it, watching goats graze doesn't make for the most exciting afternoon. By noon, even Billy found himself plopped in a lawn chair, taking a little snooze. Only the Hoove stayed by the goats' sides, tending to them like he was a born goat herder.

Billy was startled awake when two shrill voices pierced the stillness of the afternoon.

"Goats!" one screamed.

"Way cool!" screamed the other.

Before Billy could even get up from his chair, two boys had charged into the backyard through the hole in the chain-link fence that separated their yard from the Brownstones'. Both boys wore LA Kings hockey helmets and carried small hockey sticks made for eight-year-olds. They were followed by Amber, who was also carrying a hockey stick but wore a sparkly tiara in her hair and a feather boa around her neck.

"Here comes Princess Hat Trick," she sang. "I am the ruler of the Kingdom of Ice."

"Hey, guys," Billy shouted, jumping to his feet. "Take it down a notch. You don't want to scare the goats."

But Teddy and Jack Wolf were two boys who only knew how to take it *up* a notch. They came flying into the middle of the yard, circling the goats and waving their sticks.

"He skates across the rink," Jack shouted, running toward Grady, "and comes face-to-face with the goalie."

Grady's eyes grew wide with fear and he bleated loudly as Jack barreled up to him, his hockey stick orbiting above his head.

"But then Teddy comes in to defend the goal," the other brother yelled. "He body checks Jack! No score!"

The two boys surrounded Grady, who spun in a circle as he tried to follow their whirling actions. But goats weren't designed to spin in circles and after a few turns, Grady could no longer walk in a straight line and zigzagged his way over to Beatrice.

"The goalie abandons the net!" Jack screamed, shooting an imaginary puck into an imaginary net.

"He shoots, he scores!" Teddy said, raising his small stick above his head in victory. The two boys jumped up and down so long that eventually they fell down in a heap and started rolling around on the grass, while Amber twirled in crazy circles around the yard. She ran right up to Grady and in her loudest voice shrieked in his ear.

"Our team won!" she hollered. "And now Princess Hat Trick rules the whole ice rink universe!" With that, she let out a shrill scream that could probably be heard in all the ice rinks in the universe. It was more than poor Grady could take, and with a giant leap, he bolted for the hole in the fence and started burrowing through it into the Brownstone yard. Seeing him take off like that alarmed Beatrice, who followed in close pursuit.

"Hey, Grady," the Hoove called. "Don't

panic, pal. You either, Beatrice! They're just playing. That's what human kids do."

But as everyone knows, you can't reason with an alarmed goat. And before Billy or the Hoove could stop them, both goats had charged the fence, found the hole, and wormed their way into the Brownstone backyard, bleating at the top of their lungs.

Rod's mother came running out onto the back porch.

"Hey, scat!" she called to the goats. "Don't you dare eat my flowers."

But it was too late. Grady had found a bed of big blue hydrangeas and was ripping them to shreds. Beatrice was head butting the trunk of the fig tree in the center of their yard.

"Nooooooooo!" screamed Mrs. Brownstone. "Get out of my tree. And those are my prize-winning hydrangeas! Rod, come out here and help me!"

Grady didn't listen, though, and kept head butting the tree trunk, rattling it so hard that the ripe figs shot off the tree in every direction like soft, juicy missiles flying through the air. One of them landed smack on Grady's head, its juice running down into his mouth. Grady stopped dead in his tracks when he tasted the delicious fruit. Immediately his attention turned to the top of his head, and he reared up on his hind legs trying to flip the fig onto the ground. He looked like a break-dancer gone wild. Meanwhile, Rod had sauntered onto to the back porch, eating some cereal out of a plastic bowl.

"What's the problem, Mom?" he said. But as soon as he finished the sentence, Beatrice stopped gobbling the hydrangeas and set her sites on cereal. She sniffed the air. Her nostrils flared at the scent of Cheerios in milk, and she bolted toward Rod. Her hooves stomped the earth and she bleated wildly, as only a goat seeking Cheerios can.

"Whoa!" Rod yelled. "Somebody stop that goat. It's committing a 905 code violation!!!"

"What's that?" his mother yelled.

"It means it's attacking me!" he said. "Which is not only against the law, it's scaring the pants off me!"

All the color drained from Rod's face as Beatrice started clomping up the steps of the porch. Rod's hands were shaking so much that the cereal flew out of them. As the Cheerios and milk flew through the air, a generous portion landed in Mrs. Brownstone's hair.

"I just came from the beauty salon!" she screamed. "I was supposed to look glamorous for my office party tonight, but now I look like breakfast cereal!"

"You think you've got problems," Rod yelled. "Look what's happening to me!"

The other portion of the cereal and milk had spilled all over his sneakers, and Beatrice was having the time of her life licking his shoes. Rod the Bully was paralyzed with fear, pinned against the wall of his own house by a goat enjoying an afternoon snack. And now that Beatrice had licked all the Cheerios off his shoes, she was starting on the shoelaces, sucking them into her mouth like spaghetti noodles.

"I can see its tongue," he screamed. "I'll never wear these shoes again."

"Stop complaining and help me catch them!" his mother said, running down the steps and onto the grass.

"He's scared of animals," Amber yelled, twirling by the fig tree. "But Princess Hat Trick isn't!"

"Rod's a scaredy-cat!" Jack Wolf hollered.

"Big, tough scaredy-cat!" his brother Teddy echoed.

"I am not, you little punks," Rod shouted. "It's just that . . . I . . . I . . . have to call the police. This is a job for law enforcement!"

"Billy! Did you hear that?" the Hoove shouted. "The big jerk is calling the police!"

"No! Don't call the police!" Billy yelled to Rod, scurrying through the hole in the fence. "They're just goats. We'll catch them."

But that was easier said than done. Grady and Beatrice played a clever game of hide-and-seek in the Brownstone backyard, ducking behind the hedges, the toolshed, even the lawn furniture. They were impossible to catch. Every time Billy got close, Jack and Teddy would grab them around the neck and try to ride them like small ponies. This did not sit well with the goats.

Billy's whole family came over to help. Bennett tried to slow Jack and Teddy down, which was as difficult as capturing the goats.

"Boys," he said. "You cannot ride goats. That's why they do not make goat saddles."

"But we want to!" Jack protested.

"There are many things we want to do in life," Bennett explained, leaning over to look Jack right in the eyes. "For example, I would like to clean the teeth of every person in America, but that's just not practical."

Bennett was so involved in trying to get Jack to follow his logic, that he didn't see Grady approaching. Both of Grady's goat eyes were focused on only one thing — the delicious looking toupee resting like a bird's nest on the top of Bennett's head. In one swift movement, Grady shot his tongue out of his mouth and whipped off Bennett's wig, sucking the whole hairy mess into his mouth in one gulp. Bennett's hands flew to his suddenly bald head and a look of horror came over his face. That look was matched by the shock on Jack's face.

"Wow!" he screamed. "The goat's got your hair. Here, Mr. Goat, take mine, too!"

Fortunately, Billy's mom had arrived in time to try to grab the toupee out of Grady's mouth.

"Give that back, you naughty goat," she said. "It's not polite to eat somebody else's hair."

She pulled on the toupee, and so did Grady. It was perhaps the strangest tug of war in the history of human-goat interactions.

Billy had been frantically chasing Beatrice, but when he saw his mom in battle with Grady, he joined in to help. Grabbing her around the waist, he tugged hard, but Grady had dug in his hooves and was stronger than the two of them.

"Help us, Bennett," Mrs. Broccoli-Fielding called.

"I'll help, too!" Amber cried.

"Us, too," Jack and Teddy said.

Before long, a chain of six humans had formed to try to yank Bennett's toupee away from one goat. It was too much for Grady, and at last, he opened his mouth and gave up the saliva-soaked hair.

"Yay! We won!" Amber said and started twirling around the backyard again.

"Don't worry, dear," Billy's mom said to Bennett as he looked at his forlorn wig. "I'll wash it on the delicate cycle."

Breeze did not get involved in any of the goat drama. She just stood by and called various friends on her phone giving them a play-by-play of the bizarre backyard chaos.

Grady and Beatrice simply refused to be caught. And to make matters worse, Jack and Teddy Wolf, accompanied by her highness, Princess Hat Trick, continued to be fireballs of energy. Every time anyone would come close to cornering one of the goats, Jack would scream. "GOOOAAAALLLL!" and Teddy would stomp his feet and shake his booty in a victory dance, startling the cornered goat into a fit of sneezes before sending it running across the yard.

"Eeuuww," Breeze said to her friend Sophia on the phone. "I think they have some kind of nasal condition."

"It's their alarm signal," Billy said to her.

"Well, it alarms me," said Breeze.

The Hoove was the most upset of anyone. He stood on the sidelines, calling directions to Billy.

"Move quietly. You're scaring them!" he said.

"Grady's trying to protect Beatrice!" he added.

"Offer them some alfalfa!" he suggested. "Don't touch their foreheads. They don't like that."

It was a disaster. The two frightened goats tore up the yard, knocking over ceramic flowerpots, jostling all the birds out of the bird feeder, and even managing to ruin Bennett's hairpiece. And worst of all, they totally demolished Mrs. Brownstone's prizewinning hydrangeas. All the parents were upset. The three eight-year-olds were out of control. Breeze was grossed out. Billy was frustrated beyond words. And the Hoove was worried sick about Beatrice and Grady.

By the time the police car pulled up to the Brownstone house, its siren blaring, and two police officers stormed into the backyard, it just couldn't have gotten any worse.

CHAPTER 10

"Yay! Police officers!" Teddy yelled.

"Just like in the movies!" Jack screamed, high-fiving Amber. "Hanging out at your house is so fun!"

"Where's the emergency?" Officer Redding asked, urgently looking around to survey the scene while his partner, Officer Otis, inspected the porch.

"Over there!" Rod called out from his position safely inside the back door. "Those goats have gone wild!"

Beatrice was pawing at the avocado tree, trying to climb up its sloping trunk. Grady had bolted over to the Hoove and was busy ripping some climbing ivy off the wall of the toolshed. Every time Grady bleated, the Hoove would stroke his back and say, "I'm with you, Big Guy. No reason to panic."

"Goats?" Officer Redding said. "I thought you reported a house break-in."

"Exactly," Rod answered. "Those two nasty goats broke into our backyard and violated our property."

"Looks like we have a goat emergency on our hands." Officer Otis laughed.

"Who's responsible for these animals?" Officer Redding asked, obviously not as amused as his partner was.

"I am," Billy said, stepping forward. "I rented them to clean up our backyard. Goats are very earth friendly, you know."

"Well, you can't have your animals ransacking someone else's backyard," Officer Redding answered. "Earth friendly or not."

"They ate my hydrangeas," Mrs. Brownstone chimed in.

"They're a menace to society," Rod added. "You should arrest them right now. I'd come out there and make a citizen's arrest myself, but I'm boiling my shoes. They've been contaminated by goat saliva."

"Scaredy-cat!" the three little kids screamed all at once, which prompted Mrs. Brownstone to round them up and send them into the house to watch cartoons.

"We don't arrest animals," Officer Redding said. "We contain them until the proper authorities can be called."

As the two officers edged over to the goats, Bennett ran into the house to call Rent-A-Goat. He hoped that if he could get Smiley there soon, the goats could be taken home safely without any authorities having to be called.

"You collar the fat goat," Officer Redding said to his partner. "I'll nab the brown-and-white one."

Officer Otis nodded, then snapped a branch off a shrub and approached Beatrice.

"Here you go, kiddo," she said. "You look like you have a hearty appetite."

Beatrice sensed that this was not as friendly a gesture as it seemed, and looking directly at Officer Otis, let out a loud, panicky bleat. This in turn aroused Grady's suspicions, and he let loose a series of alarmed sneezes. Officer Redding reached out to grab him, but the Hoove threw himself around Grady's neck and pulled him backward. Officer Redding pulled harder and so did the Hoove. "Something's yanking on that goat," Officer Redding said, looking right at the Hoove. "And it smells like rotten oranges."

"He sees you!" Billy called out to the Hoove. "Let go!"

"He can't see me," the Hoove answered. "And I'm not letting go. Trust me, this guy does not have Grady's best interests at heart."

Officer Redding turned to Billy. "Who you talking to, kid?"

"Um . . . no one," Billy answered, unable to think of a clever explanation.

"That little creep does that all the time," Rod shouted. "I watch him with my binoculars, and he's always talking to someone who isn't there. Other strange things happen, too. Like clocks flying across his room and stuff. I think you should investigate him once you get that stupid goat locked up."

Officer Redding nodded. "I can't put my finger on it, but I sense something odd around here."

"Hey, who you calling odd?" the Hoove shouted. He let go of Grady and zoomed over to

Officer Redding, grabbing onto his pants by the belt and tugging upward, giving him a giant wedgie. The policeman wheeled around and assumed a martial arts position, ready to pounce on whoever had the nerve to wedgie him. But he saw no one.

"That's right," the Hoove howled. "You're looking at me. I did it. Next time you think about calling me odd, remember that I am King of the Wedgie."

"That's enough, Hoover," Billy said, unable to contain his words.

"Who's Hoover?" Officer Otis asked Billy. She had managed to grab hold of Beatrice, who was trying to escape her grasp.

"Oh, that's my son's nickname," Mrs. Broccoli-Fielding said. "The boys on the base-ball team call him Hoover the Mover. Isn't that so wonderfully boyish?"

Beatrice was struggling to escape, turning her head from side to side to loosen Officer Otis's hold on her horns. She let out a stream of unhappy bleats. It made the Hoove crazy to see that, and unable to restrain himself, he let go of Officer Redding's trousers and dove directly at Officer Otis's shoes. In a single motion, he untied both her shoelaces, and then tied them back together in a single knot. When she tried to take a step, she fell over onto the grass and got caught in the hydrangea plant. While Officer Redding and Mrs. Broccoli-Fielding rushed to her side to help her up, Billy got right up in the Hoove's face.

"Go to your room," he whispered. "You're making this worse. I'll handle it."

"Promise me you'll protect Grady and Beatrice," the Hoove said.

"Okay. Just disappear right now or they're going to find you out."

"How are they going to do that? I'm invisible."

"They're police officers, Hoove. They have ways. Go! Now!"

Hoover let go of Grady and gave Beatrice a little scratch on the back, then zoomed off across the yard. And with the Hoove gone, Billy was able to give his undivided attention to the task of helping the police officers calm the goats. He wanted to lure them with food, so he told Breeze to go in the kitchen and bring him whatever was in the vegetable drawer. She returned with six carrots, half a head of lettuce, and a bunch of green onions.

"I don't want the onions," he told her. "It might give them gas."

"What is it with you and gas?" Breeze said. "Is that the only thing you can talk about?"

The goats weren't afraid of Billy, and when he held a few carrots out to them, they came over to him and ate right out of his hand. His mother got some twine from the garage, and officers Redding and Otis tied two slipknots and slipped a makeshift leash over each of the goats' heads. Within ten minutes, the situation was under control. Grady and Beatrice were happily eating their vegetables, Mrs. Brownstone was picking up the remains of her hydrangea bush, and Rod was inside dictating a report to Officer Redding while Officer Otis took a report from Mrs. Broccoli-Fielding.

"We're going to have to take the goats into custody," she said. "They've created a public disturbance."

"What will you do with them?" Billy asked.

"Take them to animal rescue."

Billy remembered his promise to the Hoove.

"You can't do that," he said. "Just give us a few minutes. Please. I'm begging you."

Billy shoved the carrots and lettuce into Breeze's hands.

"Here, you feed them," he said. "I have to go in the house."

"Eeuuww, these vegetables have goat saliva on them," Breeze said, immediately dropping them in a pile at her feet. But that was okay with Grady and Beatrice. They weren't fussy.

"Bennett!" Billy called as he ran in the back door. "Did you reach Smiley?"

"He's on his way," Bennett said.

Without a word, Billy turned on his heel and sped out of the house, arriving breathless just as Officer Otis was putting her ballpoint pen in her pocket and his mom was getting up to return to the house.

"Call off animal rescue," he panted. "The goat's owner is going to arrive any minute now."

"I can't authorize that on my own," Officer Otis said. "I'll have to check with my partner."

They stood there for a minute waiting for Officer Redding to join them. He was standing at the back door of the Brownstone house, finishing up a conversation with Rod. When he came over to join them, Officer Otis told him about Smiley coming to claim the goats.

"That works out pretty well," Officer Redding said, turning to Billy, "because I actually have a few questions to ask this young man here. According to Deputy Brownstone . . ."

"Deputy?" Billy said. "Since when is Rod Brownstone a deputy?"

"Well, technically he isn't, but he asked that I call him that and I don't see any reason not to. He's got a keen sense of law enforcement, that one does."

"Yeah, too keen if you ask me," Billy said.

"Anyway, Deputy Brownstone has reported a series of unexplained events going on at your house. Flying clocks. Floating objects. Lights going on and off when no one is home. Unexplained bolts of lightning. Do you know anything about that?"

Billy was glad that his mother had already reached the back door, so she couldn't hear this conversation. She could always tell when he was lying.

"No, sir," Billy said. "Everything here is totally normal."

"So you think Deputy Brownstone is making this up?"

"I can't say, sir. All I know about him is that he's a big snoop and is afraid of lizards."

"Well, let's just say that I'm going to be keeping an eye on things here," the policeman said. "Deputy Brownstone seems like a credible source to me."

"What does that mean?" Billy asked. Actually, he had a pretty good idea what it meant, but he was stalling for time so Smiley could arrive.

"It means that he doesn't seem like a liar to me. And since my job is to protect the citizens of our community from everything — seen or unseen — I'm going to be patrolling this street very carefully from now on."

Billy gulped. Poor Hoover. First he was grounded by the Higher-Up authorities. Now he was being stalked by the Lower-Down authorities.

Officer Redding called animal rescue, who said they'd have a truck out there in half an

138

hour. Luckily, Smiley's truck pulled up just fifteen minutes later and he convinced the officers to let him take custody of the goats. He promised that he would watch them carefully and see that they didn't cause any more disturbances. Billy apologized to him and tried to explain what had happened. But Smiley didn't seem too upset. He just loaded Grady and Beatrice into the car and shook Billy's hand with a firm squeeze.

"Goats," he said, climbing into the cab of his truck. "You gotta love 'em."

When Billy went back into the house, his parents wanted to talk over what had happened, but Billy was in no mood. He was desperate to make sure the Hoove was okay and to warn him about the police patrol. They were going to have to make some new rules. So he told his parents that he had to take a shower before he could talk, because he was covered in goat-beard hair and it was making him itch. No parent could say no to that.

Billy went to his room and found the Hoove pacing back and forth nervously.

"Hoove, we have to talk about those police officers," he began.

"How are Grady and Beatrice?" the Hoove interrupted. "They didn't get hurt, did they? Poor kids, they were so scared."

"They're fine," Billy reassured him. "I told you I'd protect them, and I did."

"You're a champ, Billy. So, can I go see them now?" The Hoove flipped on his jaunty newsboy cap and floated quickly over to the door.

"No, Hoove. You can't see them. They're gone."

The Hoove came to a sudden stop and turned to face Billy. He looked puzzled.

"What do you mean, they're gone? I thought we had them for the whole weekend."

"The police were going to send them to animal rescue, so we called Smiley, and he came right away and picked them up."

"And you didn't come tell me they were leaving? You didn't even give me a chance to say good-bye?"

"I'm sorry, Hoove. It just happened so fast and . . ."

"What is it with me?" the Hoove said. "I just can't catch a break. First they took Penelope from me. And now this. I cared about those goats, Billy Boy. They liked me. I mean, really liked me. They didn't care if I was a ghost or a real boy. It didn't matter one bit to them. We were just friends."

"Hoove, I know you feel bad."

"Do you? Do you know how it feels to be all cooped up for ninety-nine years? To be constantly punished for just being you, for wanting to have a little fun? Do you know what it's like to lose every friend you've got?"

"I'm your friend, Hoove. You haven't lost me."

"Some friend. You didn't even tell me the goats were going. Just snatched them out from under me."

"But I didn't realize . . ."

"Yeah, well you just violated the Hoove's Rule Number Five Hundred and Thirteen, which I happen to have just made up right here on the spot. Friends gotta realize important stuff about each other."

Suddenly, there was a knock on the door and Breeze barged in without waiting to be invited, as usual.

"Who are you talking to?" she asked.

"Myself," Billy answered, too tired to make up a story.

"That's so wrong in every way," Breeze sighed. "Anyway, weird one, the parental units want to talk to you in the kitchen. Like immediately. They sent me to find you. So now that I've found you, I'll be leaving. Ta-ta. Oh, by the way, there's goat saliva on your shirt."

As soon as she was gone, Billy turned to continue his conversation with the Hoove, but he had disappeared. Billy went to the closet and tried to open it, but it was locked from the inside.

"Open up, Hoove," he said, pounding on the door. "Come on. We can play Monopoly. Or Nerf golf. Anything you want."

Billy knocked until his knuckles were bright red, but there was no answer. The Hoove was inside, hurt and angry, and he wasn't coming out. Not for Monopoly. Not for Nerf golf. Not for Billy.

Hoover Porterhouse III was alone in the closet, and he wasn't coming out for anyone.

CHAPTER 11

At last, Billy gave up and walked reluctantly to the kitchen. He dreaded the lecture he was sure to get from his mom and Bennett. It wasn't his fault that the goat situation had gotten so out of control, but he had a bad feeling he was going to get punished anyway. If they made him pay for the damage done to the Brownstones' backyard, he'd have no allowance until he was thirty-seven years old.

He found his parents huddled near the back door. Bennett was holding a cardboard box and his mom was looking at something inside. They didn't even glance up when he walked in, so he decided to launch into his own defense before they had a chance to accuse him.

"Hey, guys, I'm sorry about the goat incident. But I think we can all agree that I'm not actually responsible for what happened out there," he said.

"We're going to have to discuss a suitable consequence for your irresponsible behavior," his mom said.

Billy tried to read his mom's expression as she turned to him. Was this the face of an angry woman who was about to take away his allowance forever? Billy held his breath, waiting to hear what his punishment was going to be. But oddly enough, she changed the subject.

"Come see what we've found" was all she said.

Billy walked over and looked in the box. Inside was the gray-and-white cat with a pink nose and long white whiskers, the same one he had seen hiding in the hedges the day that Berko escaped. Since then, Billy had noticed that cat wandering around the neighborhood, licking itself on the branch of a tree or poking around for tuna fish cans on trash pickup day. No one knew who it belonged to, so everyone on the block just assumed it had been orphaned or left behind by a family who moved away. People were definitely feeding it regularly because it was plenty fat, especially around the middle.

"What's that cat doing here?" he asked.

"When the goats were on their rampage, she must have gotten very frightened," Bennett answered. "We found her hiding under the patio table on our porch, shaking like a leaf."

"Poor, sweet thing," Billy's mom added. "She looks so nervous. I'm sure she's never seen goats before."

"Which leads us to the discussion of consequences," Bennett said. "We need to discuss the goat fiasco."

Billy took a deep breath and prepared to hear his punishment.

"We're not angry with you, Bill," Bennett went on. "But we do feel that you need to demonstrate more responsibility toward the animal kingdom. You didn't anticipate the problems those goats could face, and as a result, you put those two fine animals at risk."

Billy's mom nodded, getting that principal look on her face — the one that says, "I understand what you're going through, but someone has to be the adult here and that someone is me."

"Bennett and I have what we believe is a great idea. We think you should look after this cat until she feels better," she said. "That would show us that you've come to understand how much we humans need to take care of our animals, whether they be goats or scared little cats."

"You mean scared *big* cats," Billy corrected. "That is one humongous feline in there."

"It's not nice to make fun of anyone's size," Billy's mother said sternly. "Besides, the goats you brought into the neighborhood disrupted this cat's life. You owe it to her to offer comfort and support."

"For how long, Mom?"

"At least until she's back to her old self."

"So taking care of her is my punishment?"

"It's an opportunity to practice responsibility," she said.

Bennett reached out and placed the cardboard box in Billy's arms. The cat looked up at Billy and let out a not-too-friendly meow.

"Be sure to keep her in your room with the door closed," Bennett said. "Breeze is highly allergic to cat dander. If that cat is free to wander the house, we'll have a mucus situation on our hands that no amount of Kleenex can handle."

There was really nothing more to say after that, so Billy took the box and headed to his room. He did stop in front of the door to Breeze's room on the way and lingered with the cat box, just to annoy her. He could hear her sneezing as he continued down the hall to his room.

"Hey, Hoove," he called out once he had kicked the door closed. "Come on out. We have a visitor."

There was no answer. Apparently, the Hoove was still sulking in the closet, so Billy got busy making a temporary home for the cat. He took her out of the cardboard box and lifted her onto a worn-out plaid flannel pillow he had brought home from Silver Arrow sleepaway camp. After giving her a bowl of water to drink and one of his many unpaired gym socks to play with, he settled down on the floor next to her.

"So what's your name?" he asked, giving her a little scratch behind the ear.

"Sssssssssssssss," the cat hissed.

"Starts with an *S.* Snoopy? Snowflake? Sassafras? Stinky? Stormy?"

The cat hissed again.

"Okay," Billy said. "Stormy it is. So tell me, Stormy, how'd you get so fat? Or should I say plump? No offense, but you could maybe up your cardio workout."

Stormy didn't understand the content of Billy's speech, but she did seem to respond well to his gentle tone of voice. As Billy continued scratching her head and talking softly to her about baseball and school and video games, she gradually started to relax. She stopped trembling and although she was not what you'd call friendly, she didn't seem horribly fearful any longer. Billy was exhausted from the excitement of the day, and before long, he nodded off with Stormy curled up on the pillow next to him.

"Hey, Billy Boy! It's gotten quiet out there. Too quiet, if you ask me."

When Billy didn't answer, Hoover floated through the closet door and into the middle of the room, not noticing Billy and Stormy asleep on the floor.

"Hey, Billy, where'd you go?" he called out.

Billy awoke with a jolt, not because of the sound of Hoover's voice, but because of the sudden change in Stormy's position. The cat was no longer curled up contentedly next to him, but was standing on all four paws, her back arched and her mouth open, exposing all her teeth. The hair on her back stood straight up.

"Relax, Stormy," Billy said. "That's just the Hoove. He's your new friend."

Stormy didn't agree. She let out a long, low hiss and sprang through the air, aiming her body directly at the Hoove. Her ears lay flat against her head and her claws were out. If Hoover had been a real person, she would have landed smack on his chest. But since he was a ghost, she flew right through him and landed on the curtains covering Billy's window. Hissing and growling and showing her teeth, she clutched onto the curtains, never taking her green eyes off the Hoove.

"She's really sweet," Billy said. "Reach out and pet her."

"No way, Billy Boy. In case you hadn't noticed, cats hate me. And I'm not a big fan of fur balls, either."

"But this is Stormy. She's going to stay here in my room."

"How many times do I have to tell you? It's *my* room."

"Anyway, you and Stormy are going to grow to love each other, I just know it."

The Hoove looked over at the cat dangling from the curtains, batting the air with her outstretched claws and baring her razor-sharp teeth. This sure didn't look like love to him.

"Hey," he said to Stormy. "Looks to me like somebody's been going hog wild on the cat chow. They should change your name to Jelly Belly!"

"She's not fat," Billy said. "She's plus-size."

"Let's call it like it is, pal. That cat looks like she swallowed a cow. Maybe the whole herd."

Just for emphasis, the Hoove puffed himself up with air until he, too, looked like he had swallowed a cow. Stormy's eyes grew wide with terror. She arched her back again, twitched her tail aggressively, and snarled at the Hoove.

"That does it," he said. "The cat leaves now. End of discussion."

"She can't leave," Billy said. "My parents say I have to look after her, to prove to them that I can be responsible to others."

"Sounds familiar," the Hoove said. "All too familiar."

"It's my punishment for letting the goats run wild in Mrs. Brownstone's garden."

"Aw, my heart breaks for you."

The Hoove raised his arms like he was pretending to play a sad song on the violin. The sudden movement alarmed Stormy, who leapt from the curtains onto Billy's bed and immediately assumed an attack position.

"Okay, okay. Don't get your tail in a twist," the Hoove said. "I wasn't coming after you. I've got better things to do with my time."

"Try petting her," Billy said. "She's had a bad scare, so she needs a little love."

There was a knock on the door and since no one came barging in, Billy knew it wasn't Breeze.

"Bill," Bennett called from the hall. "We're about to sit down to dinner. Leave the cat in her box and join us."

"No, thanks, Bennett. I think I'll skip dinner."

"It's pot sticker night. You have to come right now or the dumplings will actually stick to the pot."

"I'm really not too hungry, Bennett."

"This isn't about eating, Bill. This is about quality family time. Engaging in the fine art of conversation. Now hurry up."

Billy turned to the Hoove, who was still hovering in the middle of the room. He and Stormy were in a standoff, each glaring at the other.

"Are you two going to be okay?" he asked.

"How do I know? All the cat does is stare, like it's watching air move."

"I'll eat fast and be back as soon as I can. I'll bring a treat for Stormy."

"Better make it something low calorie," the Hoove said. "Very low. She doesn't need any more poundage or we're going to have to push her around in a wheelbarrow."

After Billy left, the Hoove floated slowly over to Billy's desk and draped himself over the chair, never taking his eyes off Stormy. Stormy stared back.

"So what's up with you and me?" the Hoove finally said, having realized you can't stare down a cat. "We can be friends or enemies, you take your pick."

Stormy cocked her head and listened carefully to Hoove's voice.

"You can hate me, but you'd be the only one," he went on. "Come on, I look good. I smell good. And if you like citrus, I'm your guy. Oh, and I tell a good joke. Ever hear the one about . . ."

Stormy squinted her green eyes at the Hoove.

"Okay, I'll save that one for later."

Stormy's ears stood at attention. She must have sensed that the Hoove was in a friendlier mood, because her body relaxed a little. Even her tail stopped twitching up and down and started moving side to side.

"But, hey, I can't resist a good cat joke," the Hoove said, putting his hands behind his head and thinking. "You're going to love this one. What does a cat like to eat on a hot day? You give up? A mice cream cone!"

The Hoove let out a laugh, and Stormy's ears really perked up. She stretched to her full length, letting the tension out of her body, and meowed.

"All right, I detect a little progress," the Hoove went on. "Okay, here's another winner. Did you hear about the cat that swallowed a ball of wool? She had mittens."

The Hoove laughed again, and this time, Stormy purred softly.

"Now we're getting somewhere," the Hoove said. "This next one's going to have you meowing up a storm. Or maybe I should say meowing up a stormy. The Brownstone creep would like it, too, although I hope you never have to encounter that bag of wind. Here goes. How do cats keep law and order?"

Stormy stared at the Hoove. It wasn't a hostile stare like before, but a curious one.

"Claw enforcement!"

The Hoove howled with laughter and this time, Stormy sprang off the bed and jumped into his lap. She snuggled up next to him and lay her head down on his nonexistent knee.

"Whoa, look at us," the Hoove said, giving her a chilly pet down the length of her back. "Aren't we getting cozy?"

Stormy shivered as Hoover stroked her, but stayed exactly where she was, purring happily.

Out in the kitchen, dinner was taking much longer than Billy expected. It was a Chinese meal, and Bennett insisted that everyone use chopsticks to eat. He was quite good at using them since he had developed excellent fine-motor skills picking plaque off people's teeth. Billy and Breeze, on the other hand, spent almost an hour stabbing at their dumplings with their chopsticks and only succeeded in sending them flying off their plates and across the table. Three times Billy asked if he could be excused, and three times his mother said no.

The Hoove didn't care that dinner was a long affair. He had stopped counting the minutes until Billy's return. He sat contentedly on the chair, just stroking Stormy's back and listening to her purr. He felt peaceful. Even the sting of never getting to say good-bye to Grady and Beatrice didn't feel so bad when Stormy was on his lap. He could have gone on like that for hours.

But after awhile, Stormy became less content. Her purring, which had been soft and gentle, became louder and faster.

"What's wrong, Storms? A tornado coming?" the Hoove asked, looking a little concerned.

Stormy jumped from his lap onto the floor. She paced around the room nervously until she found the newspaper sports section, which Billy kept by his bed. She pounced on that newspaper like it was a tasty mackerel and started to tear it into strips.

"What's gotten into you?" the Hoove asked. "I've heard of reading the sports section, but shredding it seems a little extreme — and that's coming from a sports fan."

He bent down to pick Stormy up, but she resisted him. Picking up the shreds of paper in her mouth, she carried them in little piles over to the cardboard box and dropped them inside.

"You're not a bird," the Hoove said to her. "So why are you building a nest?"

When the bottom of the box was covered, Stormy let out a loud, urgent purr and got inside. The Hoove sat down next to the cardboard box to watch her. He waited and watched, and within five minutes, he knew why Stormy was building a nest. She was having kittens.

The Hoove's eyes grew as big as flying saucers.

"Hey, wait a minute!" he yelled. "You're having mittens! I mean kittens! You can't do that! I don't know the first thing about delivering mittens . . . kittens . . . little cats."

But Stormy didn't need the Hoove's help. Her motherly instincts were perfect, and she knew just what to do. One by one, she delivered her babies, and when it was all over, there were three little kittens in the box, a gray one, a spotted one, and a white one.

The Hoove reached out and petted their wet, newborn heads.

"Hey, little fellows," he said softly. "Welcome to the world."

Stormy reached out and licked his nonexistent hand with her sandpapery tongue. By the time Billy came back from dinner, the Hoove was grinning from ear to ear, like a proud new father.

"Billy," he said. "I have amazing news."

"You got ungrounded?" Billy guessed.

"Even better," the Hoove answered, his voice full of emotion. "We have mittens!"

CHAPTER 12

Billy and the Hoove sat on the floor by the cardboard box for a long while, watching Stormy take care of her brand-new kittens. They were so tiny and weak, but even though their eyes were closed, they still were able to snuggle up right next to their mom.

"So I guess this explains why Stormy was so fat," Billy said.

"Plump," the Hoove corrected. "And might I mention, you would be, too, if you had three whole animals inside your belly."

"I'm going to tell my mom and Bennett," Billy said, but the Hoove shook his head.

"Let's name them first. I think we should call the gray one Thunder, the white one Lightning, and the spotted one Raindrop."

"That's pretty weather oriented, Hoove."

"Well, her name is Stormy, so if you ask me, I think it's perfectly appropriate." He reached out and stroked the little white one, who squeaked like a tiny mouse. "Although maybe I should name this one Penelope, after my goat. She looks like a Penelope."

"Hoove," Billy said gently. "Maybe it's not such a good idea to name the kittens."

"Why not? We can't just keep calling them Hey You."

"Well, when you give something a name, you get more attached to it, and then when we have to give them away, we're going to feel really bad."

The Hoove's head actually spun around three times on his neck.

"Wait a minute," he said. "What you just said made my head spin. Why do we have to give them away?"

"Well, for one thing, Breeze is allergic to cats."

"Fine, we'll give Breeze away."

"We can't have four cats here. That's just crazy. There'd be cats running all over. And there'd be no one home to take care of them. It wouldn't be responsible of us to keep them if we can't take good care of them."

The Hoove got up and started pacing around the room.

"Responsibility," he grumbled. "That word just won't leave me alone. It's getting on my nerves."

The Hoove floated back over to the kittens and leaned down to stroke their heads. Then he sighed a big, ghostly sigh, flew to the closet, and went inside, slamming the door behind him.

"You okay?" Billy asked through the door.

"It just stinks, that's all. Go get your parents. Do what you have to do."

Billy went and got the rest of the family. His mom and Bennett were thrilled to see the new kittens, and even Breeze said they were pretty cute . . . until she got a sneeze attack so bad she nearly blew herself down the hall.

"I was hoping we could keep them," Billy said to his mom and Bennett, even though he knew what the answer would be.

"They can stay with us until they're old enough to leave their mother," Mrs. Broccoli-Fielding said. "That will be about six weeks. Then we'll try to find them good homes."

"Couldn't we just keep Penelope?" Billy begged.

"Who's Penelope?" Bennett asked.

"The white one. She's named after someone very special."

Billy's mom reached out and gave him a hug.

"You're a sweet boy, Billy Broccoli. And you've got a big heart. I love that about you. We'll tell whoever gets her that her name is Penelope."

When his parents left, Billy went to the closet and opened the door. The Hoove was lying on the top shelf, just staring up at the ceiling.

"I tried, Hoove," Billy said.

"Yeah, I heard."

"At least we can have them for six weeks. They'll have to stay in our room because of Breeze, so you can have lots of time to hang out with them."

"Would you mind closing the door?" the Hoove said. "I'm thinking here. No offense, but you're blocking my brain waves."

Billy closed the door and got ready for bed. After he brushed his teeth and changed into his pajamas, he went to the box to check on the kittens one more time. All three were cuddled up against Stormy, and she was licking them from head to tail. Billy turned out the lights, got in bed, and fell asleep to the sound of Stormy's happy purring.

Even though the next day was Sunday, Billy woke up early. There was a commotion in his room, and he rubbed his eyes to focus on the Hoove hunched over his desk, deeply engrossed in some kind of art project. There were large sheets of paper laid out all over the floor, and every one of Billy's markers was spread over the desk top.

"What's going on, Hoove?"

"Making signs," the Hoove answered. "If we have to do this, I'm going to see to it that we do it right."

He picked up one of the sheets of paper and held it up for Billy to see. It said:

FREE KITTENS!

ONLY AVAILABLE TO GOOD, LOVING HOMES!

WE MEAN IT!

The signs were written in different colors, with drawings of cute little cats around the edges.

"I thought about this all night," the Hoove explained while he completed a cat border in navy blue. "We'll plaster the neighborhood with these signs. People will come and check out the kittens, which will give us time to observe them and pick the best families. I don't want my kittens going to just anyone, you know."

When Billy showed the signs to his parents, they were very pleased.

"This is an extremely responsible thing to do," his mother said.

"How about if I get out my trusty, surefire staple gun," Bennett said, putting a supportive hand on Billy's shoulder. "We can go out and staple these up around the neighborhood. And, Bill, as a special reward for your responsibility, I'll let you squeeze the staple gun trigger. Trust me, it's a thrill."

"I wish I could bring a friend," Billy said, feeling a little guilty about getting all the credit for something the Hoove had done.

"Your friend can come along," Bennett said. "When it comes to stapling, the more the merrier, I always say."

"Thanks, Bennett, but he can't come. He's grounded."

Billy and Bennett went on a staple-gunning extravaganza and within an hour, the FREE KITTENS signs were posted all over the neighborhood — on their block, in the supermarket parking lot, at the park, even in the window of Fur 'N Feathers. By afternoon, there were at least ten people who had lined up to see the kittens. They waited in the living room, while Billy brought them into his bedroom one at a time. The Hoove sat on the window with a clipboard, taking notes. The first person to arrive was Amber Brownstone.

"Oooohhh, they're such cuties," she squealed. "I want one."

"No way," the Hoove said. "She might be okay, but I won't have one of my kitties in the same house as her mutant brother."

He wrote down *A. Brownstone* and made a check in the NO box on his list.

Mrs. Pearson from the house on the corner was the next to arrive. She immediately bent down and tickled the spotted kitty under the chin.

"Oh, you look just like the cat I had when I was a little girl," she cooed. "How I loved my little Speckles." Billy noticed tears at the corners of her bright blue eyes. "I'd love for that little darling to come live with me. I'd name him Speckles Two."

Billy looked over at the Hoove.

"I'm liking this," he said. "Plus, she's got a good location at the corner of the block. Perfect for visitation rights."

The gray cat went to Hugo, who ran the taco stand. He said it was his daughter Maria's sixth birthday in a month, and the thing she wanted most was a cat.

"Thunder will make an excellent birthday present," the Hoove said, checking the YES box on his list. "And we know he'll always be well fed if Hugo brings home leftovers from the fish tacos."

That left the white cat, Penelope. The Hoove rejected three people in a row. The Schwartz family was moving to San Diego in a month, and the Hoove thought that was too far away. Fred Park lived in a one-room apartment and the Hoove didn't like the idea of Penelope being cooped up. The O'Donnell family was perfect, except they insisted on naming her Fiona after their Irish grandmother and that was a deal-breaker for the Hoove.

The fourth person to apply for the white cat was none other than Daisy Cole herself, the owner of Fur 'N Feathers. The minute she saw the little white kitten, she let out a high-pitched shriek.

"Oh, if she isn't the sweetest thing in the world," she squeaked. "I'll take her and bring her to the shop."

Billy looked over at the Hoove, who shook his head no. "She'll sell her," he said, "and that's definitely not okay with me."

"I'm sorry," Billy said to Daisy. "We don't want to sell Penelope. We want to find her a good home."

"Penelope!" Daisy said. "What a perfect name for her. And I have no intention of selling her. She'll stay with me at the store during the day, and go home with me and Robert at night."

"Who's this Robert character?" the Hoove asked suspiciously.

"Robert's a parrot," Billy said.

"Why, yes, dear, I know that," Daisy said. "And a very musical one at that."

Billy glanced at the Hoove, who was holding his pencil in midair, thinking.

"She wouldn't be lonely, that's for sure," he said. "And she might enjoy a retail environment."

When Daisy explained that Penelope could play on the Tower of Power cat gym she kept in the shop, the one with a tower, a rope, and a cave, that sealed the deal for the Hoove.

"The Hoove's Rule Number Sixty-One," he said, nodding. "A proper exercise regime is essential for good health and good looks."

He checked the YES box, and Billy told Daisy that she could pick up Penelope as soon as she was ready to leave her mother. They had found homes for all three kittens.

For the next four weeks, the Hoove barely left Billy's room. He brought Stormy fresh water and bowls of milk. He changed the newspaper in her box. He made little toys for the kittens out of socks and shoelaces and feathers. Day by day, the kittens grew and prospered. They learned to see and to walk. They didn't seem to mind one bit that the Hoove was a ghost. When he petted them, they'd rub up against his nonexistent finger and purr. Maybe it was the orangey scent they liked. Maybe it was the cool breeze that surrounded his hand. Or maybe they could feel a loving presence in their midst.

On Monday of the fourth week, Billy was in his room doing homework after school while the Hoove was playing with the kittens, bouncing a Ping-Pong ball against the wall and watching them bounce up and down along with it. There was a knock on the door, followed by Breeze barging in. She was holding her nose.

"Your mom asked me to give you this," she said, handing Billy a white envelope. "It was on the kitchen counter."

"Why are you holding your nose?" Billy asked.

"Because if I don't, I'll do this." Letting go of her nose, she produced a sneeze so loud it almost shook the roof off.

"Here," Billy said, handing her an entire box of Kleenex. "Sounds like you could use these."

"By the way," Breeze said, blowing her nose vigorously. "It says Hoover on the front of that envelope. Your mom says that's your nickname from the baseball team."

"It is."

"Then how come no one ever calls you that?"

"Oh . . . well . . . um . . . it *used* to be my nickname. Hoover the Mover. We've changed it."

"To what? Rufus the Doofus?"

"The door's that way," Billy said. "Don't forget to use it."

Breeze sneezed her way out, making a giant dent in the Kleenex box before she even reached her room. Billy brought the envelope over to the Hoove and stood next to him while he opened it. The page inside was blank at first, then suddenly, there was a flash of fireworks and the room filled with smoke. When the smoke cleared, Billy watched in amazement as giant French fries, the size of baseball bats, floated out of a transparent bag that seemed to glow blue, green, and lavender.

Billy poked the Hoove in the ribs.

"French fries," he whispered. "That's a positive sign."

"You never know with these guys," the Hoove answered.

He waited nervously as the French fries floated out of the bag and formed themselves into letters midair. It seemed to take forever, but then, French fries have never been known to move quickly. Finally, the message was complete. It said:

RESPONSIBILITY:

EXCELLENT PROGRESS. KEEP IT UP.

P.S. YOU ARE UNGROUNDED.

Billy jumped up and down and clapped his hands as the French fried letters disappeared into the cosmos.

"You did it, Hoove! Without even trying. You became responsible."

"Just from taking care of the kittens?" asked the Hoove. He was as amazed as Billy.

"Sure. No one in the world, living or dead, could have looked after Stormy and those three little guys better than you. You never left their side. But now you can!"

"I can go out into the world and strut my stuff," the Hoove said, automatically smoothing back his hair and flexing his biceps. "Look out, Earthlings. Here I come."

Without another word, he zoomed out through the window. Throwing himself into hyperglide, he whizzed around the neighborhood, dipping and diving through the air with his newfound freedom. He somersaulted across Moorepark Avenue, slalomed around telephone poles, and cruised over treetops. In less than thirty seconds, he was back at Billy's house, and came whooshing in the window like a rocket.

"That was fast," Billy said. "Don't you want to stay outside for a while and do anything you want?"

"You mean like tickling Brownstone behind the ear so he bats himself in the head like he's got an itch he can't scratch?"

"Yeah, something like that."

"Already did that. It was fun, but not as much fun as this."

"As what, Hoove?"

"Staying right here, taking care of Stormy and the mittens, doing just what I've been doing. Truth is, there's nothing better."

And settling down on the floor next to the

cardboard box, Hoover Porterhouse III reached out for Stormy and her kittens, rubbing their heads, scratching their ears, and happily listening to them purr.

It was music to his nonexistent ears.

Read on for a sneak peek at Billy and Hoover's next crazy adventure!

GHOST BUDDY

NEVER DANCE WITH A HAIRY BUFFALO

Using all of his ghostly strength, Hoover hooked his invisible arm through Billy's, flipped himself into hyperspeed, and yanked Billy across the art room into the hall.

Billy looked around. All he saw were four kids from his class, supervised by Mr. Wallwetter, practicing for the bow and arrow demonstration. Rod Brownstone took aim and let go of the arrow just as Billy arrived. It wobbled through the air and landed on the floor, about four feet short of the target.

"That was all your fault," he barked at Kayla Weeks. "You bumped my arm."

"See, isn't that amazing," the Hoove said to Billy.

"I don't see anything amazing," Billy answered. "Just Brownstone being a bully, as usual."

The Hoove turned to Billy and looked closely into his face.

"You don't see her, do you?"

"Kayla? Sure I see her. It's hard to miss that whole mess of red hair."

"No, I mean *her*. Standing next to Kayla. With the beautiful brown eyes and shining long black hair."

"You must be seeing things, Hoove. There's no one there but the teacher and four kids from my class. And no one has long black hair. Unless you count the hair on Mr. Wallwetter's arms, which I'd rather not."

"Concentrate, Billy," the Hoove said. "Feel her presence. Listen for the sound of her voice. And let me know when you see her."

Billy closed his eyes and concentrated. He didn't expect to see anything — he was just doing as he was told to get the Hoove off his back. But then, after a few seconds, he thought he heard something. It was a faraway rattle, like pebbles rolling in the sea, following by a faint drumbeat and the sound of a girl's voice, chanting a strange melody. He opened his eyes, and saw her — a Native American girl, about his size, with long black hair and skin so transparent that she seemed to glow.

The minute she saw Billy gazing at her, an expression of fear darted across her face. As quickly as she had appeared, she disappeared into thin air, leaving nothing in her place but Brownstone's yapping voice.

Who was she? Where did she come from? And where had she gone?